Maryan George lives with her husband and two children, plus four cats, in a 'picture postcard' by the Norwegian fjords. Teacher, composer, arranger, conductor, musician, and author, she spends every free minute writing on her stories and working on new ideas and plots. And in between, she tries to pursue her hobbies, playing in diverse bands, and being with her family.

I would like to dedicate this book to my family, who all have a fascination for the horrible, inexplicable, and unexplainable, in varying degrees, of course. My husband, without whose help, especially in the house, I would not have had time for my passion: writing and telling stories! My sister, who has more than once spent a whole evening in my company, with bottles of wine, and a good film on TV, or discussing the latest books we've read. My children, for encouraging me, and cheering me on when I doubt myself, sometimes. I love you all, and this book is for you!

Maryan George

THE THUNDERING SILENCE

AUSTIN MACAULEY PUBLISHERS™
LONDON • CAMBRIDGE • NEW YORK • SHARJAH

Copyright © Maryan George 2023

The right of Maryan George to be identified as author of this work has been asserted by the author in accordance with sections 77 and 78 of the Copyright, Designs and Patents Act 1988.

All rights reserved. No part of this publication may be reproduced, stored in a retrieval system, or transmitted in any form or by any means, electronic, mechanical, photocopying, recording, or otherwise, without the prior permission of the publishers.

Any person who commits any unauthorised act in relation to this publication may be liable to criminal prosecution and civil claims for damages.

This is a work of fiction. Names, characters, businesses, places, events, locales, and incidents are either the products of the author's imagination or used in a fictitious manner. Any resemblance to actual persons, living or dead, or actual events is purely coincidental.

A CIP catalogue record for this title is available from the British Library.

ISBN 9781398479371 (Paperback)
ISBN 9781398479388 (ePub e-book)

www.austinmacauley.com

First Published 2023
Austin Macauley Publishers Ltd®
1 Canada Square
Canary Wharf
London
E14 5AA

My love for the gruesome, the horrible, and the inexplicable, I owe to those many authors of the genre that have captivated my imagination, piqued my curiosity, and left something growing in the dark recesses of my mind. None mentioned, none forgotten.

In addition, I owe a lot to my children, for always including me in their discussions about which horror film is the best. This has included a fair bit of watching films, and in that process, I have found that peeking into someone else's imagination can be terrifying. So, yes, I have lost some sleep because of this, but the joy and enlightenment I have gotten, far outweighs that. And, yes, they are both in the book, somewhere.

Finally, an extra huge 'Thank you!' to my daughter, for once again providing me with the cover art for my book. You are one of my great inspirations!

Table of Contents

Introduction	12
Chapter 1	19
Chapter 2	36
Chapter 3	51
Chapter 4	65
Chapter 5	79
Chapter 6	103
Chapter 7	118
Chapter 8	131
Chapter 9	147
Chapter 10	160
Chapter 11	171
Chapter 12	188
The Thundering Silence	204

They say that when writing, you should always start with that which you know well, so in this book I have gone all in, and set it in the landscapes where I grew up and still live. Nordheim is a fictional place, but its similarities with many of the villages around the Sognefjord will ring a bell with the reader, and as for myself, it has a strong resemblance to the place I call home. The nature features can be found in the vicinity, and many of the folk tales related in the book, are actual folk tales or fairy tales from the area.

However, the experiences of Bridget's grandmother, are actual stories I heard my grandmother tell me, stories about happenings that she experienced as a young child. She maintained that the stories were true, and she was scared of Huldra, and other creatures from the myths and sagas, until the day she was no longer with us. Other stories, like the ones about the teeth in the water, are completely products of my imagination (I hope).

So enjoy your journey into the West-Norwegian scenery, myths, folklore, and village life, both its quaint and dark sides, and perhaps, when you have come out the other side, you will look at it a little differently?

— Maryan George —

Introduction

The morning was absolutely gorgeous; Clear, blue sky, a few white fluffs imitating clouds, but which would be gone by mid-morning, dazzling sunshine, warm—nearly hot—temperature, and a forest teeming with life; birdsong, flowers, and small as well as large animals. And to think that only yesterday it had been raining, no, pouring, windy and completely horrid.

Martin was walking up the steep slope, his breath coming in little gasps as he climbed. God, he loved this feeling, and in this weather, nothing could be better! Reaching the plateau where the ground levelled out—at least as level as it got in these parts—he spotted the ruins of some old farmhouses and sat down with his back to one of the walls that were still standing. These cottages would have been used in summer, he knew, for the milking of cows, sheep, and goats and as living quarters for the herders, usually young girls, who were looking after the livestock that was let up in the mountains for summer pasture. He looked out at the view from his seat; fantastic! About ten metres away, the plateau was cut short by a cliff, the sheer drop being over hundred and fifty metres, he had read. He was considering going over to take a peek at the drop, but he was a bit unsure how his head would feel about it, so for now he decided to just sit and enjoy the sunshine.

This was one of the things that had fascinated him since he first heard about the Norwegian mountains and the Norwegian way of co-existing with nature and the elements. It was evident in the masonry still standing, the people who built this, had taken nature and weather into consideration, and made use of the stones available to them in the terrain. The result was buildings that were still standing. The only things that had decayed or been destroyed, were the roof, the doors, and other wooden building parts. These building techniques were part of a tradition that still held, even in modern times. They had stone cottages in the Alps of course, and the techniques were similar, but not exactly the same. He had seen a documentary about it when he was seventeen years old, and now, twelve years later, he was finally here. Having done the country from north to south, this was his last stop before leaving for Paris in four days. He felt sorry that he had to leave, but he would be coming back, no doubt about that. His experiences had just fanned the fire in him, and now he dreamt of a little farm perhaps, in the mountains, with enough livestock of various kinds to get by, and with vegetables and grain in his own fields. He closed his eyes and let his daydream take flight. In his dream, he had already acquired the little farm, and was now working on the surroundings, forming, and shaping them so they would fit with the image he had in his mind. There was a shelf right at the bottom of the steep mountain side a little further up, which he had seen on pictures taken by a fellow tourist the night before, and with a little bit of work, that would be the perfect place to have his farmhouse. Just think of the view!

"Magnifique!" he muttered, almost in a daze by now, with the pleasant surroundings, myriads of little birds singing, and the clear, blue sky above him.

While he sat there, enjoying the sunshine and the cool breeze, he became aware of a deep sound, a tone or tones of sort, right at the brink of hearing, almost inaudible. It came from everywhere and nowhere at the same time, not unpleasant, but mildly intriguing. It did not go away, however, it just kept getting more and more insistent. In the end, it got to be irritating, and as the sound kept growing in strength and audibility, he realised that he could hear voices in it. He could not, as yet, discern any words, but it was clear that they were not issuing a greeting. There were growling and hissing, intermittent with the voices—which all appeared to be mingled and jumbled while speaking a language he did not know—and now it was really getting to his nerves, so he rose to his feet, facing the forest behind him, looking for the source of the sound. This forest consisted of pine and birch, mostly, with an undergrowth of ferns. The undergrowth was so dense in places that the forest appeared to have a blanket of green over its roots.

He could not see anything, so he started to pace back and forth, too nervous now to sit still, and actually scared of going into the forest to find the source of the sound, which now had reached quite audible levels. Anxious, he called out; "Show yourself! This is not funny!" Too late he realised that putting put a blanket invitation to whatever was there was maybe not the smartest thing to do, but perhaps it would not have mattered after all. The trees were moving, being whipped around as if there was a tornado, but nothing could be seen, only heard. Frightened beyond anything he had ever felt before he could only stand there, frozen, and watch in horror as the wind increased, the voices grew to a deep-throated roar, as they came closer and the movement in the trees grew wilder. When the wind hit him, it felt like a wave, crushing and drowning him, sending him helplessly flying through the air.

As he flew across the clearing, he suddenly remembered the cliff and realised he was over the edge. Hanging in the air for just a split second, he had time to take in the view of the village down by the fjord, and the depth over which he was floating.

Then the spell broke, and flailing, screaming in terror and fear, he plummeted to his death. As his death scream faded, lost in echoes, the wind subsided, and the forest fell quiet and peaceful again. Not a sound, aside from the twitter of birds, could be heard, not a thing could be seen. The world was tranquil, once again. The trees returned to their usual unmoving, calm state, and the bushes resumed their occupation of gently rustling in the lazy breeze.

In the nearby valley, Sofie, a young farmer, was repairing a fence that had been trodden down. She was a little bit irritated, because she thought it was not the cattle which were responsible, this was the result of unregulated wandering in the fields and forests. If only people would use common sense and stick to the marked paths, then they would all get along just fine, but no. Muttering under her breath, she drove down the new fence posts and got ready to fasten the wire fence to the frame. That was when she heard it, a long, terrified, absolutely horrifying shriek echoed around the mountains before ending with a sickening thud. Standing still as a statue, the only thought that ran through her mind, was, *not again…I hope it is not anyone I know…*

On top of the mountain, where there was a lake, known to be teeming with trout, a man was setting up his rod and tackle, getting ready for some relaxing hours by the water. With the weather this beautiful, he doubted if he would catch anything at all, but the beauty of this pastime, was that the trip and experience was more than half the enjoyment. He lived in a nearby town and had heard stories of the fish that could be caught in this lake, since he was a teenager. As one of the things he enjoyed most in life, was to explore new fishing arenas, like this lake, he had decided to take the day off and go on an outing. He had brought a garden chair, a well-filled picnic basket, a pair of binoculars, and even a book, so he was all ready for a quiet, lazy day, just the fish and him.

Sitting down and settling in, he noticed some odd ripples on the water, but at first did not think much of it. It could be anything, from the breeze that was occasionally rising up, to fish swimming close to the surface. He opened the thermos of coffee and drew a cup. Leaning back and facing the sun, he closed his eyes, but it did not take long before he opened them again, Was that a splash? Looking out over the lake's surface, squinting to see properly, he could clearly see the rings in the water, where evidently a sizeable fish had just landed after springing into the air. *Wow, I would like you to visit my hook!* he thought and smiled. He grabbed himself a sandwich from the basket and chewed thoughtfully on it, while he emptied his coffee cup. While he was bending down, putting the thermos back in the basket, he heard a splash again, and this time it was loud. "What in the…" He jumped in shock and surprise. "Wonder what kind of mammoth fish they have here!" He stood up this time, looking intently out on the water, searching for the rings. When he finally saw them, he got a little uneasy; the rings from the jump were far over on the other side of the lake, and for them to have made such a loud sound, whatever had made them would have had to be seriously big.

His body was starting to itch. As a veteran from the UN forces in Lebanon, it was a known reaction to him, and one he was accustomed to listen to. What made him make up his mind was, when he saw dark streaks beginning to form in the water where the last jump had been, dark streaks that seemed to converge and mingle. In a short minute, he had gathered all his belongings on his back and was headed back to the track. He could feel eyes on his neck, and he could hear the thing in the water—whatever it was—swimming toward the bank where he had been sitting just a minute ago. If anyone had told him that you could walk up the mountain and over the edge in just twenty minutes, he would have laughed at them, but now he found you could, if you were fired up by pure terror, that was. And then he almost stopped in his tracks. He had left his best rod down by the water's edge! He almost turned back, in fact he was starting to turn, when an awful sound caught his attention. It was like no sound he had ever heard before, nor did he ever want to hear it again. A low, almost inaudible growl, accompanied by a sound he had heard before, in the Middle East.

The sound of sabres being sharpened...His feet sped up the mountainside and carried him over the top and into the next valley. Behind him, he could hear what sounded like knives—or teeth—being rubbed against each other, but curious as he might be, no force on or off this planet could have made him turn around and look.

Chapter 1

In the country of Norway, the nature vistas and beautiful sceneries come by the dozen. There are in fact so many gorgeous spots, that it would be hard to pick one as the 'winner', as there will always be contenders for this title. However, the fjords along the west coast are a hot candidate, and Nordheim was clearly on or near the top of the list.

Nordheim was a tourist destination and had been so for the last 150 years. The influx of tourists had always been good, some years even great, but for the last decades it had been steadily increasing. The people who wanted to visit Nordheim had a bit of travelling to do, though, because the ways of getting to Nordheim had not developed along with the demands of modern tourism.

Travelling to Nordheim meant you were in for the long haul, even on a problem free day when everything was running on time. First, it was the long drive or bus ride on what could only be described as winding roads along the main fjord, and second, it was the nearly two-hour long ferry ride along the fjord arm, stretching almost 30 kilometres north, from the Sognefjord. This fjord did have some curves, bending this way and that in long, slow lines, but the general direction was due north. On the way, one would have ample time to admire the tall and steep mountains clad in green, topped with white, and with hundreds of small and large waterfalls cascading down the mountainsides. On a sunny day, all the tourists had to do, was lean back in their deck chairs, and admire the landscape in all its glory.

At the end of the journey, however, there it was. After the ferry ride between the tall and imposing mountains, sort of leaning over you and making you feel strangely like an ant, you would be rewarded by the opening-up and the feeling of freedom as the vista of Nordheim became visible to you. Turning around a bend in the fjord, there it lay, looking like a pearl or a diamond maybe; beautiful blue sky, wide green fields and pastures, tall mountains, decked out in green of all hues, and covered in immaculate white snow on the peaks, a fjord of deep green—almost emerald—water, and the glacier, white and turquoise blue. It took your breath away, pure and simple, and it took Toby as much by surprise as it did when he was a child, even though he knew it was coming.

He stood there on deck, relishing the air, fresh and clean, almost without any trace of pollution in it, and taking in the sights that he recognised from his last visit. That had been some years ago, when his father was still alive, and they had visited his grandfather, Olaf. He had had a lot of fun, he remembered, and Olaf had been a very atypical grandparent; He had been joyful, playful, and totally oblivious of any age-constraints as to behaviour; playing football, stealing apples from a neighbour's orchard, and going fishing for crayfish and crabs in the middle of the night, for example. Of their visits to the village, he had no clear recollections, but he remembered a busy shop with all kinds of things you could possibly need (and some that he could not imagine anyone ever needing), smiling faces at the post office, and several horse and cart equipages ready to take tourists who arrived with the ferry, up to the glacier. Yes, it had been grand, but, sadly, it had also been the last time he had seen Olaf, although he had spoken to him regularly on the phone after that trip.

Now Olaf was dead. That piece of news had been broken to him over the phone.

The police officer who had been on the other end of the line had been both compassionate and gentle, but it still was a cruel shock. He remembered having to sit down while the voice of the policewoman informed him what had happened. Olaf had died in an accident—a fall from a cliff—while on his usual morning stroll walking in the forest, and as Toby was his closest living relative, he was notified of this before it appeared on the news. It turned out that he had inherited Olaf's house and belongings—much to his surprise, although perhaps it should not have been, he was after all the only direct descendant Olaf had had—and now he was coming to Nordheim to take possession of the house and decide what he wanted to do with it.

He had stopped at the solicitors on his way, as they had offices in the small town, only a half hour drive from the ferry's departure point. When he had signed all the papers and received the necessary documents, everything was settled, and he was now the proprietor of a house.

As the ferry started slowing down, he was looking at the little village that lay there, sparkling like a gemstone in the sun. It looked so peaceful, so restful, and tranquil, that he felt his shoulders relaxing and his whole body responding to the feeling of quietness that seeped through it. *Not that it is completely quiet, of course!* he thought to himself, remembering tales of youthful daredevilry and high-risk projects. The thought made him smile.

While the ferry docked, he was looking around, searching for Roger. He had thought he could spot him on the quay, but now he was not so sure. They had been children when they last saw each other, and people change over the years. Roger, being the same age as Toby, was one of his four living relatives, the great grandson of Olaf's first cousin, Thormod. *Not exactly a close relative, but still a relative after all!* Toby was thinking to himself. Then he caught sight of someone that looked awfully familiar. He waved cautiously and was instantly rewarded with a huge wave in return; yes, that was Roger, no doubt!

When they met on the dock, the feeling of companionship was instantly there in the hug they shared. It felt like they had been apart for less than a month but were very happy to see each other again. Toby was surprised at how much Roger resembled the child he had been, the same twinkling eyes, the same quirky smile, and the same rugged frame. They embraced again and then they looked each other over, searching for signs of the children they had been.

Laughing at himself, Roger said enthusiastically, "Welcome back to Nordheim, Toby. It has been a long time since you were here, but as you can see, it is essentially the same as it was!"

He then proceeded to ask Toby if he had had any supper. When Toby told him that he had not had the time for anything besides travelling that day, he was promptly invited back to Roger's house for a bite to eat and something to drink.

It was a no-brainer of a question, of course he said "Yes, thank you!" After he had accepted the invitation, Toby and

Roger walked the few hundred metres, to Roger's house on the south side of the village. It was a rather new house, built in the 80s, with a large open living room, a kitchen with a dining space in it, and different floor levels which had been the craze at that time. Toby thought to himself that he would have to watch out if he was going to cross those floors while drunk, or in the middle of the night, or both. They sat down at the nice dining room table and had dinner, halibut, beautifully prepared, with an excellent white wine to go with it. During the meal, they took the opportunity it offered to catch up on each other's doings and plans over the last years. They had both been full of ideas for their future when they were younger, but as with most people, they found that their plans had changed—sometimes with intention and sometimes out of sheer good, or bad, luck.

Their talk turned to the affairs of people of Nordheim, and what prospects they still had for the future for both of them. Roger for example, had never considered himself a gardener, nor a farmer for that matter, but in spite of this fact he was the heir to a farm in Nordheim. Not a huge one, mind you, a modestly sized one, but a farm, nonetheless. It had therefore been with a pang of bad conscience that he had informed his parents about a year ago about his lack of interest at taking over the farm. His father's and mother's disappointment at this, was understandably considerable, and they both encouraged him to think more closely on it before making his final decision. But they both also realised that farming had become an increasingly unstable and dwindling source of income for a young man, and therefore they had begun talking about leasing the farm out to neighbours who were in search of more pasture or production areas. Meanwhile, Roger was still trying to find out what he wanted to become, which proved to be a real challenge. Lately, he had begun to narrow it down though, but he was careful about keeping it a secret. As he told Toby, "If I want the whole village to laugh themselves to ruptures, then I might consider telling them, but for now I hold my tongue!"

Toby, on the other hand, was a city boy, educated at the university. He held a degree in—in his own words—patchwork, having bachelors first in archaeology, then in astronomy. "Hmm," Roger said, "you have studied the past and then the possible future. What about the present?"

Toby laughed, blushing a little; "Well…You could say that my present is on hold," he answered. As Roger had already told him, this was also the case with him.

"Two cases of hiatus in the same family, hmm? Beginning to sound like a curse!" Roger said and laughed at himself.

While sitting there, enjoying the peace and quiet on a full stomach, they agreed that Toby would be staying with Roger for the duration of his stay. It would give them an opportunity to catch up on and renew their old friendship, and for Toby to have someone to ask all the questions that he might, or rather would, have as they moved along. After their inner animals had gone to rest, they decided to go to Olaf's house—now Toby's—and look around. They walked there, as there were no roads to the house; it lay a little distance up in the mountain side, with a beautiful view of the village, the fjord, and the glacier.

Their walk took them through the village centre as the house was situated to the north of the village, and Toby was eagerly taking in the sights along the way. There were the two hotels, of course, the eldest over a hundred years old and the other one rapidly approaching that same age. They had been started when the need arose to cater for the flood of tourists that suddenly began to come. Historically, following the industrial boom, many people, especially from the middle class, suddenly found themselves more well off than before, and they went searching for peace, quiet, and adventures, things they did not find in the bustling city life in London or Berlin, for example. When the tourists first started coming, this was mainly a summer phenomenon, but the times had changed, and the needs and wishes of the tourists as well. The two hotels were now open all year round. That meant, in other words, that they did not shut, even when winter hit, with storms and darkness.

Of old, Toby knew, they used to close in September and open again in April, due to the tourists and what they expected, or what preferences they had, but that was before the age of modern-day exploration and extreme tourism. This urge to explore and challenge yourself, had also led to the establishment of some businesses offering guided tours and kayak rental, and a few other services, like ice wall climbing, rafting, and skiing expeditions to the mountain tops, complete with off-piste downhill run going home again. As Roger said it, "Looking for experiences out of the ordinary," he explained to Toby, "people will come to walk on the glacier and climb the mountains even when the thermometer reads minus twenty!" Shuddering, feeling the cold creep into his body by just the mention of it, Toby could not for the life of him even imagine what they got out of it.

While walking along the main street, there was really only one street, Toby found, much to his surprise, that there was also a pub in the village. It had not been established the last time he had been to Nordheim, but he thought from the looks of it, it was doing reasonably well. Already at this hour, in the middle of the afternoon, there was a respectable crowd of guests sitting at the tables outside. He expected there were more inside, although it was really too nice outside to spend your day inside a dimly lit pub. Passing the village shop, open for business, they came out on the other side of the village, where roads went to the valleys and homesteads on the northern side.

They reached the path up to Olaf's house and started the climb, for it was decidedly a steep path, and when they reached the house, both men were out of breath. While they waited outside to "let it catch up to them," they took in the view.

First, they looked at the house, a sturdy house built in timber and meant to last for generations. The walls had a dark, red colour, while the windowsills and the door were painted eggshell white. Then they turned and took in the view of the surroundings. The forest was all shades of green, from the dark green of the pines and spruce trees to the moss green of ancient asps and the leaf green of the birches.

Together with the flowers, where all the colours of the spectrum could be found, it was like a symphony for the eyes. As Roger described it, "It is gorgeous, that is the only word that is fitting; gorgeous!" After a moment he added, "And in a way heart-warming."

Toby nodded his agreement, adding a little epithet of his own; "It looks like home!" With their breathing now under control, they entered the house.

The interior of the house was clean and well-kept, although filled with papers and opened books and magazines on every available surface. One thing hit Toby though, everything seemed like it had been cut out of a museum catalogue. All the furniture and other articles of decoration, plus all the household appliances, were from a different century.

"But they all still work!" said Roger triumphantly when Toby remarked on this. "The stove and the refrigerator are probably the newest items in the house."

"I can see that," Toby answered, "and I remember it all! I had just forgotten how many lovely pieces of furniture he had here." Rummaging around in the kitchen for a while, they made up their minds to start properly in the parlour.

There they commenced their exploration of the house. The first thing they found, was that the dust had already begun to settle on the shelves and lamps. "It is amazing how fast a house loses its lived-in feeling," Toby mused.

Roger nodded, "Yes. It has not been more than two weeks since Olaf passed away, and already the house is taking on that empty appearance."

"On the other hand, it might all be in our imaginations," Toby added.

Looking questioningly at him, Roger asked him what he meant.

Toby smiled, "It was in a lecture at the university, about a year ago, that one of my professors spoke about what the expectations we carry around in our subconscious do to our perception of events or things that we encounter."

Roger thought about that for a second, then nodded his approval, "A wise man. I had not thought about it that way, but it makes sense to me!"

Talking about the topic for a couple more minutes, they then decided to get a move on and check out the house before it got too late, and they were too tired.

Having sneezed their way through the parlour, they then continued to the living room, taking books out of the shelves and putting them back after a brief examination. *There seemed to be an inordinate number of books about or from the paranormal area,* Toby thought, *and they ranged from sensationalist, I, the victim of a shaman! to the parapsychological research files, and everything in between.*

"Wow," he exclaimed, "he was quite into these things, wasn't he?"

"Yeah," he heard Roger answering, his head down in a basket full of magazines, "and he was the original 'original'."

"What the village poison tongues called 'the village idiot', but he was far from an idiot, I can tell you that!"

"Oh, I believe you!" Toby replied, "I was only here as a little boy, but even then, I remember Olaf as kind, childish in a way, but very, very sharp. Village idiot, indeed! I would like to have a talk with the people responsible for those kinds of rumours! I think I would be able to teach them a thing or two about tolerance!"

Roger, who had at this time re-emerged from the basket, smiled at that but said in a still voice that Toby could barely hear, that he should be careful what he wished for, as these people were never far away from where things were happening, lurking in the shadows and observing.

While they looked through the rest of the ground floor; taking another trip to the kitchen, and then the bathroom, making only a cursory check and intending to come back the next day, they realised that if there were any interesting bits, books, or belongings, these would probably be further up or into the house—in other words, on the first floor. They went up the stairs together, chatting and laughing. When they reached the landing, they saw that there were only two rooms up there, and since it was getting to be evening, they therefore decided to start at opposite ends of the house, to be more efficient. Toby went into the room at the northern end of the house, which proved to be Olaf's bedroom. It was neat and tidy, as well as being uncluttered, which was more than could be said of the living room or parlour, he thought to himself with a smile.

It did not take him long to find something interesting, a photo album. In it were pictures of family and friends, and the vistas or scenery in the surroundings, holiday trips, and, of course, the usual celebrations; Christmas, Easter, birthdays, national days, and so on. He was looking at the pictures of himself and his father on their last visit, loosing himself in fond memories, when he felt something behind him. Turning around, expecting to see Roger, he was surprised at seeing absolutely no-one.

Nothing was there, not even a speck of dust. Wrinkling his brow in confusion, he turned back to the album. In the back, among the most recent pictures, he found several pictures of a girl, or rather a young woman, with a sweet smile, whom he was not familiar with. Trying hard to focus his memory to see if he could come up with something Olaf might have told him in one of their—rather prolonged—telephone conversations over the last years, he still came up empty. In the pictures, she was holding books more often than not, and looking rather studious, so he wondered if she could be a student of something or other, visiting Olaf as part of her research. It had happened before, he knew. His attention was diverted, however, when he, once again, had the sensation that he was not alone. Someone was peeking over his shoulder, while breathing gently next to his face.

Turning quickly around to catch the culprit, he was again left with nothing.

Whatever had disturbed him was invisible as well as inaudible. *A ghost, perhaps?* That thought sent a little thrill down his spine! Getting up and searching the room intently with his eyes, he decided that he had had enough for one day. Going out of the room he called for Roger, who came quickly to the door of the room he had been in.

"Have you noticed someone or something else here?" Toby asked.

"No," came the answer, "but I have found something very interesting."

He was holding two books in his hands, that proved to be Olaf's diaries. Looking briefly through them, Toby decided to bring them and the album with him and peruse them more thoroughly at leisure when he was back at Roger's place. Summers this far north are never dark, but by now it had gotten dim outside, as it was nearly midnight. Roger suggested that they would call it quits for the night, and that they could make a stop at the pub; sit down, have a beer, and talk about the things they had found (or just things in general). The pub was on their way home, after all!

"Amen to that!" answered Toby, and so it was decided.

Upon entering the pub, they noticed first of all that it was full to the point of bursting, and secondly, that there was a tiny space in the very back of the room that was vacant at the moment. Roger made his way to this spot and slid in there like quicksilver, while Toby bought two large beers at the bar and followed him, carefully carrying the two full tankards while trying to avoid bumping into people on his way to the back. Having successfully made the journey, he placed one glass before Roger, before manoeuvring past the table—a tight squeeze—and sink into his own seat.

When in place, he then raised his glass and they toasted each other's health, drinking deeply. With a sigh of content, they both set their beers down, looked at each other, and burst out laughing.

"A lot of dust just got washed away from my throat!" Roger said.

Toby smiled and confirmed that he had the same feeling. "It felt almost like a rebirth," he said, "I feel born again, after spending the whole afternoon peeking into someone else's life. But it has been interesting, that's for sure!"

"Agreed!" answered Roger.

Their talk turned to their findings, starting with the discoveries on the first floor. They both wondered about the young woman in the photos, but neither of them could come up with a name for her. Roger thought aloud, "Could she be connected to the big topic of Olaf's life, the paranormal?"

"She is hardly a ghost." Said Toby. "If she is anything, she is a researcher or student."

"Or a witch!" laughed Roger.

"Wouldn't that just be the thing for you?" Toby answered in the most juvenile body language he knew, and the two laughed fit to split.

Intrigued by the noise the two were making, they soon had a rather large crowd gathered, joining in the merrymaking. Several of the people they met that night were friends or acquaintances of Roger, old schoolmates, neighbours, and such. One fellow, named Thor, was the first to open his mouth and ask if they wanted company, but others soon followed suit. Thor did not belie his name, being clearly both taller and wider than average, and with a booming voice. As he was also constantly on the verge of erupting in laughter, he proved to be good company for the remainder of the evening. Ansgar was another of the youths sitting down, and he could actually remember Toby from that visit long ago.

Toby was astounded at this, "Wow! That is almost like that politician, the one who could remember things that had happened before he was born!"

Ansgar laughed fit to split but managed to gasp out, "How young do you think I am?"

Toby replied "Well…fourteen?"

The rest of the evening went on in the same vein, the laughter coming in uproarious waves and the comments flying.

Toby could not help himself, he had to study these new acquaintances with his observer's eye. It had become an ingrained habit during his years of study and something he found both amusing and informative. He noticed that they all wore dungarees and sweatshirts or T-shirts, and that the most common footwear was sneakers. Nearly all of them looked like they knew everything there was to know about tractors and how to use them, but he could not see, nor hear, many linguists or students of astronomy in the group. *Although*, he thought to himself, *that sounds more like a snob talking than a scientist. Better watch it!* As they talked, most of the conversation wound its way through familiar territory; crops, livestock, expectations for the harvest, the hardships and benefits of farming, who was seeing who, and who was getting hitched. Toby was, in short, given a thorough introduction to the life in the village, both inner and outer, and he enjoyed it.

After some hours of this, Toby felt the same way as he did before an exam, he had a head crammed full of information, but he had nothing to pin it on yet, thus feeling totally bewildered and ready to make his getaway. It proved to be difficult, though, because the pub had taken on the characteristics of a boat, swaying quite forcefully at times.

To top it off, he had seemingly developed a hearing problem, with everyone talking in low, slow voices and sounding like Scar, the brother of Mufasa, on half speed. By now, they were discussing football, a topic Toby was only slightly interested in, but which had a very high standing with the locals. He had no idea how many times someone had asked him about his opinion on the local team, and how he thought they would do in the run-up of the season. He managed to get out of it by muttering some nonsense and toasting their health. Fortunately, the level of intoxication was now at a stage where this was a solid strategy. The whole group was by now singing supporter songs and making sincere promises of everlasting brotherhood, united in the sacred name of football.

In short, they had a grand evening, and went home to Roger's around three thirty that night, weaving their way along the road. They also had some off-road trips. "Ooof," came the grunt from Toby when a ditch magically appeared under his right foot, and sent him reeling.

"Hahaha! Ai!" came the answer from Roger, who made a mysterious disappearance when the left ditch proved to be steeper than he thought.

Thus, the two cousins entertained each other on the way home, using the ditches on both sides of the road until they eventually found their way to the house. As they were preoccupied with walking or putting one foot ahead of the other without entangling them, neither of them noticed the sound of soft footsteps following them up and then inside, just a few steps behind them.

As the two of them went to sleep, or rather went into alcohol-induced forgetfulness, Sofie, the young farmer, was having trouble sleeping. Every time she got close to falling asleep, she would hear the scream from the dying tourist as he fell to his death. Mingled with his scream were the screams of others who had met their fate at that cliff.

Sofie herself knew she had heard six of them, including the last one, Olaf. Shaking her head, she got up to get a glass of water, but ended up getting a glass of whisky instead. She knew it was a dangerous path to go down, it might help, initially, but it made sure you ended up with a mighty big monkey on your back if you kept on that path. Deciding that it was a thought for later consideration, she went back to bed, and was rewarded when half an hour later, she sank into blissful sleep.

Her dreams, however, became far from blissful as the night wore on, and around five o'clock in the morning, she awoke with a scream in her throat that could have woken the dead if it had been released. As it were, it almost choked her, keeping it in, but eventually she was able to sit up and draw a deep, shaky breath. Though the sigh of relief that she expected, turned out to be a flood of tears. After a while, crying helplessly into her pillow, she dried her tears, still shaking, and wowed silently to herself never to talk about it to anyone, and to get out while she still could. As she did not remember her dream, she was unable to say what was so scary about it, but just thinking of it, brought her close to panic and tears again. "Enough is enough," she mumbled to herself as she got out of bed, put on her clothes, and went downstairs to make herself a bucket of coffee.

Chapter 2

The night passed without incident, at least as far as the two men, or logs, were concerned. The only thing that happened to them both, were incredibly vivid nightmares. Other than that, they did not register a thing, and as the nightmares had vanished by the time they woke, all they could remember of them afterwards, were the funnier parts; Roger falling off the bed and nearly getting his head stuck under the bedframe before clawing his way up again, and Toby crawling into his duvet cover and almost panicking before finding his way back out. The only thing they might have wished for, was that the night could have lasted just a little bit longer.

The next morning dawned much too soon, and as they both had windows facing the east, the sun looked in on them at around six o'clock. It appeared to be in wonderful shape and a terrific mood, drenching the two somewhat grumpy men in sunshine.

Roger half-jokingly referred to waking up that way as "the morning after," when they both awoke with a sore head, and a feeling of nausea. Nursing these carefully with a smoothie, based mostly on raw eggs, plus coffee, they both eventually made their slightly wobbly way out on the porch, tottering like old men. *We look like a pair of old geezers*, Toby thought, wobbling around on arthritic legs in the warm—soon to be hot—morning sun. He snickered and giggled a little at that, but then his head told him to pipe down.

Roger tentatively made breakfast, consisting of eggs, bacon, tomato beans, and cocktail sausages. He did not expect much of it to be eaten, but to his surprise it all vanished. Toby was careful with his first bites, but then the wolf-hunger struck, and soon he was gobbling it down like a champion. Roger followed suit, and in no time at all, the breakfast was gone. Feeling good about himself, he settled into a garden chair placed on the porch and enjoyed the sunshine and the feeling of his dwindling headache.

Toby, who was occupying another chair on the porch, was also feeling a lot better, but something was clearly bothering him, or getting on his nerves. He had a feeling that there were flies or rather midgets, those tiny little devils, in the air, attacking the back of his shoulders and neck, which led to him incessantly reaching behind his neck and slapping at these spots, without catching a single one of them, of course. Roger, who found this rather amusing, was laughing at his futile attempts at being a sort of human flyswatter.

"Invisible hornets? Attack of the killer wee?" he joked, fighting to keep control of giggles that threatened to burst into a gale of laughter.

However, he choked on his laughter when he suddenly saw something that effectively made his eyes open wide. Behind Toby, he could see the line of the forest, edging up on his garden. The boundary between the two was rather diffuse, as his garden tended to be a bit on the wild side. Sometimes he could happen to see a deer in the clearing in front of the forest, and sometimes hares and foxes would make an appearance, but what he was now seeing...he refused to believe what his eyes were showing him!

On the border between the forest and his untended garden, stood a figure whom he easily recognised, a man, tall and well-built, and with a straight back and a strong posture, despite his years. He was so clear that Roger almost greeted him without thinking. The only problem was, the man that stood there in the bright morning light, was dead. He had been dead for over two weeks, in fact, and this simple fact could be the explanation for Roger's reaction.

Roger cried out "Olaf!" in a shocked and strangled voice. As his body jerked with the shock and the power of his exclamation, he spilled his coffee, burning his leg without noticing it. The look on Roger's face made Toby, who was sitting with his back to the forest, whip around in his chair, and so he was rewarded with a glimpse of the apparition before it melted away in the air. The sudden movement on his part unbalanced his chair, however, so it crashed to the porch, thereby sending his coffee and cup in two separate directions and spilling Toby out on the porch steps.

Fortunately, the coffee and the cup landed on separate sides of Toby, so he escaped any burns, but the feeling he got from his lower back told him there was a good chance he should avoid sitting down for prolonged periods of time that day and maybe the next as well.

Getting up and brushing himself off, he studied Roger's face with anxious eyes.

Roger still had a wild, surprised look in his face, and his eyes were frantically searching the edge of the forest, looking for fresh signs of the ghost he had just seen. Toby grabbed him by the shoulders and turned Roger's face toward him,

"Was that Olaf?" he asked in a slightly quavering, high-pitched voice.

"Yes…" came the answer, with disbelief in his voice, as if Roger was doubting his own eyes. In a way, Toby supposed, he was, and quite naturally so. It was not a common thing for anyone, not even a professional ghost-hunter, to see an apparition or ghost, and especially not in broad daylight.

Thoroughly unsettled, Toby set his chair back on its legs, and sat down cautiously. Sitting there, fundamentally shocked, both men remained silent for what seemed like an eternity. In reality, it probably only lasted a few minutes, but due to the plasticity of time, it felt much, much longer. If they could have shown each other a film of their thought activity while they sat there, it would have looked like an abstract chaos, both in sound and colours.

When they finally snapped out of it, they looked up and met each other's eyes. Toby broke the silence in a voice that did not seem to be his own, saying, "So it was really…"

His face still expressing shock, all Roger could do was nod affirmatively. Then he opened his mouth, "Yes…it was. He was really there, although that is an impossibility! He could not have been!"

The last words exploded out of his mouth, and in turn this acted as a catalyst for them both, unlocking the flood gates and setting lose a stream of questions that were bottled up inside. They were questioning everything they had just experienced, beginning with what they had seen, or imagined they had seen. Was it really a ghost or something else, how was it possible, how could it be explained, and how it most definitely could not be believed, or?

"Do you believe in ghosts?" Roger asked, bewildered.

"No," came the answer, "not until three minutes ago, anyway!" Toby was shaking his head.

"I cannot believe it now, either, but I saw what I saw!" Roger's hands were shaking as he tried to fill his cup again and sounding like a man trying to convince a true sceptic, which he probably was, namely himself. "Could there be other explanations?" he wondered, holding his cup steady with both hands.

"Possibly…" Toby replied, "but I can't think of any right now."

Discussing the occurrence at length, their conclusion was that, firstly, they had seen what they had seen, and neither one of them was suffering from hallucinations.

Secondly, they concluded that Olaf must have something of importance to convey to one of them, most likely Toby, his heir. Thirdly, they also found themselves to be completely out of their depth in this, as none of them had any expertise in the field of spirit-talking, ghost hunting, necessary witchcraft, or wizard-battling for that matter. To sum it up; they needed help—whether professional, new age style, or scientific—or all three, as Toby remarked—or the problem would remain unanswered and unresolved.

When at last they felt ready and up to it, they started out on the walk to Olaf's house, back through the village centre. Compared to the previous day, they were quiet while walking. Not because they had nothing to say, but because they had too much. Toby needed something to distract him, just so he could get some distance between himself and the shock he had just had, so he started to study the landscape around him. What he saw, nearly made him lose his breath again, but for very different reasons. The aforementioned tall, imposing mountains lined the sides of the deep, green fjord. The mountains were all clad in dark evergreens, like fir and pine, as well as several other species of trees and bushes, growing all the way up to the snow-capped peaks. On top of the mountains to the north was the glacier, glittering like a jewel, all turquoise and white. The sight of all this, together with the colourful patches of wildflowers in the foreground, made his brain go into overdrive, as he silently told himself. He started to laugh at himself, making Roger turn around and look at him.

"What?"

Shaking his head and smiling, Toby explained his line of thought and concluded, "I realised that I was sounding like a robot! It is short-circuiting my sensory input! How weird is that?!"

"Sounds like a stone-hard realist trying to explain the beauty of an impressionist's painting," growled Roger good-humouredly.

Once again, they started the climb up the hill. Before long, both of them were breathing hard and holding their sides. The path up to Olaf's house was exactly as steep as it were the day before, but it still felt both steeper and longer.

On the last, hard climb up to the house, they spotted a woman standing in front of the porch, smiling at them, as they came along the path. She was pretty in a natural way, with flowing, auburn curls, halfway down her back, big brown-green eyes, a nice complexion, and a body fit for hikes and trips in the wild. She also looked a little whimsical.

Her wardrobe was as colourful as the summer itself, green shorts, and a yellow, frilly top, which made her look very young—*almost like a teenager*, Toby thought. He could say for sure that he had never seen her before, but still there was something familiar about her, although he could not say what it was.

However, as they got closer and he got a clearer look at her, something dawned on him, "That's the girl from the photographs!" he hissed to Roger as they took the last steps up to the porch.

Smiling brightly, she came forward to greet them, and introduced herself as Sandra Billings. She explained that she had been a close friend of Olaf over the last five years, and that she was also a fellow 'weirdo' or 'nutter' in the eyes of most of the village inhabitants.

"Shall we go inside where it is cooler and have a sit-down?" Toby asked, still panting a little.

"Out of breath?" Sandra asked, with a little smile.

"Yes," Toby answered, "completely winded!"

Laughing, she followed him onto the porch and into the living room, with Roger bringing up the rear. There they all sat down and enjoyed the comfort of the deep, soft chairs that were placed around the low, oval table in the middle of the room.

"So," Roger started, "you and Olaf were friends and fellow conspiracy makers?"

Sandra's laughter that greeted this question, was contagious; a brook let loose down a mountainside. To not join her, would have been impossible, so they soon followed suit, and whatever awkwardness that might still have been there, vaporised into the clear air.

"Well," she said, "I suppose you could say that, at least from a certain point of view. But I prefer to call us investigators into the hush-hush realm, more commonly known as the dark side, or the paranormal if you are of a scientific bent." She ended, smiling again.

Toby asked, serious now, what exactly they had been doing, and what ideas they had been working on.

She looked thoughtful for a moment before answering, "Oh, well. I've been laughed at before, so I'll survive being laughed at again," she said, and then she went on to tell them. She was a student, as it turned out, with anthropology, archaeology, and folklore in her degree. *Sounds like a female version of Toby,* Roger thought to himself. Olaf and she had connected, she continued, when she approached him to get an insight into the stories, sagas, and fairy tales of the area.

Explaining the ideas and concepts that Olaf and she had come to share, took a while, especially with all the exclamations of "What?", "No!", and "I don't believe it!" from the two men. She started by introducing them to the history of the area, a lot of which Roger was familiar with, but it also revealed some parts that were completely new to him. As the two had gotten to know each other, Olaf had revealed to her that he had a research project; 'Inexplicable deaths and what could be behind them.' From what she told them, the thing that had put Olaf on the track of something sinister, was all the unexplained deaths over the centuries. There did not seem to be any explanation that fit them all, so he started looking into other, alternative explanations to find the answers. When he started up, he thought it would be a case-by-case study, all with different agents. But that was until he took a closer, in-depth, look at the history of his own neighbourhood. Numerous deaths kept piling up, all without a clear reason or explanation, but all of them somehow connected. He had developed a theory, she told them, but he kept it close to his chest, for obvious reasons.

The theory involved mythological creatures, such as Noekken and Draugen, both beings that live in water, as well as gods from the Norse mythology. There were many of them, and quite a few had something to do with water, rivers, lakes, ponds, brooks, and the sea. Snow and ice were also represented in this company.

Of course, Toby thought to himself, that would make perfect sense to a people surrounded by mountains, fjords, rivers, et cetera, in the summer as well as the winter. Oh, and the glacier, we cannot forget that! Included in this universe were also paranormal beings like the ghost that Roger and Toby had seen that morning. Some of this was familiar territory to them both—*New Age concoctions of ancient superstitions,* Toby thought, but some of it was downright outlandish and ludicrous. This included the way that these diverse creatures were viewed as part of the same package, so to speak, even though they were considered to belong to different ages as well as religions.

Balderdash was a good word for it, Toby thought. At least that was what he would have called it, had she not been so candid and serious when she laid it out for them. Sandra, sensing their disbelief and internal struggle regarding what she had to say, just smiled, and remarked that she was used to this reaction; people were too pre-occupied with what they thought or, more importantly, believed to pay attention to what was really there.

Roger and Toby, who had both felt their resistance to what they thought were wild ideas rising in them, smiled ruefully. Then they looked at each other, and with a sigh Toby answered her, "Well, if it had been 24 hours ago, I would have hit you with a broadside of university arguments as to the validity of what you just told us, but my usual reply of 'Balderdash!' has been put out of commission. You see, we had an unsettling experience this morning." Her eyebrows forming a puzzled expression, she looked questioningly at him.

"We...We were sitting on the porch of Roger's house, nursing a well-earned headache, when...Well...He looked behind me and...Oh, hell! We saw a ghost!" Toby's hands were sweaty, and his face was red, and at this point he was certain that the ridicule that Sandra had been talking about, was about to hit him in the face. He could feel Roger cringing in his seat next to him.

The response he got was downright flabbergasting, "Oh, who did you see? Was it someone you knew? Olaf perhaps?"

Her matter-of-fact tone made them feel both stupid and dizzy with relief.

When they had regained their composure, as well as a normal colouring, the sense of relief in the room was tangible. Sandra smiled at them, an open, friendly, and knowing smile, and suggested that they should sit out in the sunlight on the porch while they discussed their encounter.

"Somehow," she said, "it seems that daylight and especially sunlight, can scare away the fog of misinterpretations when it comes to ghostly apparitions. They are most of the time not the fearsome ghouls they are made to be in films and books!"

Getting up and going out into the sun, they were astounded at the strength of the sunrays; it hung there in the sky, bathing everything it reached in a hot, shimmering shine, making them relax even further. They sat down in that dazzling sunshine on the porch, in Olaf's old and comfortably worn rattan chairs, moulded after the many buttocks that had sat in them.

When they started talking, they were hesitant at first, all of them a little uncertain about the others regarding what they knew about the topic, how they would react, and so forth. But when they got started, their discussion soon became both enlightening and interesting. As it turned out, Sandra had a lot of knowledge about ghosts, both first-hand and second hand, and she proved to be an expert on the many ways of how they could or should proceed with the communication. She agreed with Roger in his assumption that Olaf's ghost had a message for Toby, and so they ought to try to speak to him, somehow.

Now, it was an unknown world they were heading into, at least for Toby and Roger, and therefore they both welcomed her advice and guidance in the matter. When they had told her about the encounter in detail, she first gave it a moments consideration. Then she suggested that they hold an old-fashioned séance to see if Olaf was willing to come to them, and tell them what he wanted to convey, and why. It was obvious that it was something of importance, otherwise he would have been content just watching them from the other side, she said to the two, now rather wide-eyed men.

As they were already sitting in the shabby and worn, but very comfortable chairs on the porch, she suggested that the séance should take place there. There was a small, round table standing on the porch, bearing the marks of many a glass and cup over the years. Toby and Roger got up from their seats and put it in between the chairs as a centre-point. On it, she placed a candle and then lit it. It did not illuminate the day, in fact its flame was hardly visible, but she explained that this made it easier for the spirits to focus. Toby and Roger followed these preparations with keen interest, even if they were a bit puzzled, but none of them said anything.

After they had settled back in their chairs again, she explained the usual procedure in a séance and then asked them if they had any questions. Toby, who knew about séances from both his studies and from student pranks, could not help but asking the question that had been forming in his mind.

"Excuse me, but should it not be dark before we try this? I have always heard that the 'communication lines between this world and the world beyond will only function when aided by the force of darkness', as the mediums claim."

Sandra's laughter rang free and trilling once again, "Oh, dear me! That is so gullible it is sweet! Someone has been preying on your kiosk-literature approach and prejudice!"

Blushing and feeling slightly like a fool, Toby concentrated on the task ahead of them. Roger, who had been about to voice the same question, was only happy that he had kept his mouth shut.

They just sat there in the sunlight for what seemed like an eternity, eyes closed, and hands joined, feeling ridiculous—at least Toby and Roger did—and Toby was just about to call it a futile attempt, when something odd happened. He felt, or sensed, his left hand being jerked. The grip was that of an old but hale man, and it was insistent, not threatening. It was the strangest sensation, and he did not have the slightest idea what to do, how to react, or to respond to it. Fortunately, Sandra did.

Toby was holding hands with Sandra on his left-hand side, and she had also felt the tug of another hand on his. "Open your eyes slowly," she said softly, "and say 'Hello' to an old friend."

Very slowly, Toby opened his eyes. First, he looked down at his hand where he felt the pressure from this unknown presence against his skin. What he saw was something incredible; a firm, strong hand, and yet only the image of a hand, without...substance to it? He shook his head. The confused rambling in his mind only made matters more difficult to understand, or perhaps it was a clarification of him really not getting it? Or...could it be that he was in denial? Looking up, he looked straight into a face he knew, and the surprise jolted him slightly. Then the apparition smiled; a smile of such warmth and joy that Toby forgot everything about his confusion and smiled back. He felt emotions began to stir inside him; intense happiness mixed and mingled with regret. Then, a flood of emotions suddenly hit him like a tsunami, powerful enough to make him lose his breath for a second. All the feelings that had been locked up inside after he had been informed about the accident, broke loose, overpowering him, and making him cry before he could control himself. Regret for all the years he had lost while he was busy playing at being student and being 'serious', wasting time by prioritising less important activities. But then joy took over, and with it came memories that had been buried deep, although never forgotten, memories of brighter days when he was a boy and his grandfather was with him, and they could just enjoy being alive. The memories from those happy and carefree days in his childhood made his eyes sparkle with tears again, but now they were tears of happiness, and the joy of seeing a friend that he had not expected to ever meet again.

Roger, who had opened his eyes in that instant, uttered a small "Oh!", and the ghost of Olaf Larsson turned its head slightly to smile at him too, before turning back towards Toby. Olaf also nodded courteously to Sandra, and acknowledged her assistance with a smile, but it was Toby that he focused on, that much was clear. Olaf, although perhaps slightly older than Toby remembered him, looked remarkably like his old self, an elderly gentleman, a gentle giant of a man, with a mane of thick, curly hair. In fact, Toby thought, he looked exactly as the man Toby remembered from his last visit all those years ago. Somehow, he must have conveyed all his feelings to Olaf, for he could distinctly see the ghost smiling a little mischievously, the way he used to when he was up to something a little shady.

Then he became conscious that he did not just see Olaf, he saw through him! And on the heels of that thought came the obvious, *Of course you can see through him! He is a ghost, and they are often transparent!* As this internal conversation played out in his mind, he could see Olaf wink solemnly at him, and he could not help but smile; *Oh, yes. This was Olaf, all right!* Then another thought hit him, *He can read my mind, I think, somehow!*

The conversation that followed, with a lot of help of Sandra as medium, was mainly between Toby and Olaf, but Roger was also included. Firstly, Olaf wanted to know as much as possible about Toby, his life, his whereabouts, and his plans. Roger was just getting around to comparing Olaf with a village gossipmonger when Olaf turned his attention to him. Blushing and stuttering he managed to cough out some answers to the barrage of questions that Olaf had, mostly about his family, and then he fell silent-partially from exhaustion, partially from embarrassment at his inadequate answers.

Even with Sandra as a more than competent medium, this conversation had its difficulties or quirks. *It is almost like radio back in the day,* Roger thought bemusedly, *bad connection and all!* when the questions and answer part started to slow down. Now it was Toby's turn to ask questions, and the one question he really wanted to ask, was, "What is it you want to tell me?" Paradoxically, the ghost went absolutely silent, and for what seemed like an eternity, all that could be heard, or felt was their pulse, thundering in their ears. The silence lasted until they felt ready to scream, but then Olaf started to speak again, slowly, almost chanting the words. Toby and Roger, both expecting to hear something about papers that had been hidden away, or something buried that needed to be found, were totally unprepared for what Olaf said, and at first did not get very much out of it. It seemed like a typical children's rhyme to begin with, but as it progressed, it started to take on a decidedly freakish nature. The ending was what they would both remember afterwards, "Stay clear of his paths if you are wise, or the thundering silence will mark your demise. When the world falls quiet, then you will hear. When silence descends, you must be aware. For the wind will blow and the sun will sting, and fear and sorrow will both take wing." As the last words faded away, Toby became aware that his grandfather was also fading, getting absorbed into the sunlight. The last glimpse of him that Toby caught, was his sorrowful smile, and his eyes, brimming with tears.

Chapter 3

Toby kept staring at the spot where Olaf had been standing only seconds before, for a very long time. All sounds in the surroundings seemed to be cut off as if a huge pair of scissors had just cut the tape, and left them in a silent film; except in colour. It felt as if the world itself was holding its breath, waiting for Olaf to make his reappearance. But when this did not happen, brute exhaustion took its toll, and he slumped back in his chair, feeling like a wrung dishcloth. The other two were just as exhausted, Sandra maybe most of all, so they both followed suit. All three of them were totally bereft of energy, barely able to lift their eyes, at which point they would just gaze into the sunlit day without any enthusiasm whatsoever.

Sandra sat with closed eyes for a while, then she opened her mouth to speak. After a hoarse croak, she decided it was probably a better idea to start with a glass of water. When she had emptied the glass, she put it down, then tried again, this time slightly more successfully. "If you feel as washed-out as I do right now, you do not have to be troubled about it, it is perfectly normal. You see, a ghost or apparition needs a lot of external energy to appear in front of people's eyes, and the brighter the scene, the more energy they need. That is why they are seldom seen in bright daylight, Toby, not that they are children of darkness." Toby blushed a little, but he was glad he had gotten an explanation. Then Sandra asked if any of them had understood the message in the rhyme. She was looking directly into Toby's face when she asked, and for some reason this made him blush again. *Thank the sun for camouflage!* he thought.

When he answered in the negative, she turned her attention to Roger, but he looked as nonplussed as Toby. Then, as if it were pre-arranged, they both turned to Sandra and looked her straight in the face, "What about you," said Roger, "do you have any idea what he meant to tell us?"

At first, Sandra got slightly uneasy, feeling the weight of their intense stares, but then she laughed, and whatever had been in those stares, promptly vanished. "How can you expect me to know?" she asked. "We were friends and fellow researchers in the paranormal, but when it comes to the rhyme, I am as stumped as you are."

Toby and Roger looked briefly at each other, then, both of them started talking at the same time. After a moment's confusion, which Sandra listened to with a little twinkle in her eyes, they both shut up at the same time, before Toby nodded to Roger, indicating that he should start. Roger began by asking if it could have anything to do with the house or any belongings of Olaf's. Sandra thought it over for a little while, but then she said, "No," and added that she would find that very unlikely. The most paranormal thing that existed in the house, aside from the books and papers dealing with the topic, was a crystal ball.

Toby was just sitting there, listening to this exchange, while he studied the pines behind Olaf's house.

Approximately 100 metres from the house, the pine forest started its climb up the steep, majestic slopes of the mountain. Dark, evergreen trees, standing still and silent in row upon row, almost organised, but not quite. *It looks peaceful* he thought, *almost serene...* Then he added in the same moment. *But it can also be dark in there. Dark and forbidding.* If he remembered correctly, it could be unpleasantly cold and dim inside the pine forest.

Turning back towards the others, he asked abruptly, "Could the rhyme have something to do with whatever you and Olaf were working at, or looking for?"

Startled, Sandra looked into his eyes. She frowned, looking as if she were going to deny that, then her eyes widened just a little and she nodded slowly. "It might..." she said, "but I do not know how to interpret the rhyme, if not...There is someone we can go and see." They looked at her in silence, questioningly. "There is a man, with whom Olaf spoke frequently. He is a researcher and self-proclaimed ghost hunter slash myth abolisher, and he might be able to help us unravel what Olaf meant with that rhyme."

"Where can we find him?" asked Toby.

"He is staying at the Hotel Daleswood," she answered, "and his name is Kenneth Barker." With this statement hanging in the air as a signal, they got up, gathered their belongings—phones, keys, and general stuff—and started on their walk back to the 'town' centre in search for Kenneth Barker, as Hotel Daleswood lay in the village midst.

During their walk to the hotel, they were given a quick rundown of the hotel's history by Roger. It turned out to be both fascinating and engaging, and as the trip was much too short for the whole story, Roger promised that he would tell it in full that evening. He contented himself by giving them an overview of the timeline, from the time it was built at the end of the nineteenth century till the present day, the family running it, and, of course, the ghosts that were said to abide there. There were a few of them, and they all seemed to have some sort of connection with the family and its male members. Although Roger had meant for this last part to be funny, the ghost that they had just had a conversation with made the possibility of more ghosts something they were reluctant to take on, one was enough in the course of a day, and they had met him twice!

Going down the hill was a lot easier than going up, Roger concluded, as they reached the village in about half the time, compared to what they had used going up. The quick stroll through the centre of the village had a lot of sights in it, from tourists eating ice-cream and trying to shield it from the seagulls to children swimming in the emerald-green waters of the fjord itself.

"Brrr, that looks cold!" Toby remarked, making Roger smile.

"Yes, it is!" he confirmed, "Somewhere around eight degrees Celsius I think!"

Sandra said nothing, but she shuddered visibly.

When they reached the hotel, Sandra went inside to ask for Kenneth Barker while the other two waited outside in the sunlit garden. They spent their waiting time admiring the building, a rather impressive wooden building, looking almost like a fairy-tale castle, complete with a round tower on the north-east corner of the building. The garden surrounding it was nicely kept and looking fashionably old.

When she came back out, she told them that she had been informed—no less—by the receptionist that Mr Barker was currently doing research in the local churchyard.

"The face he put on when he said that, made him look as if he smelled something nasty!" Sandra said indignantly, as they went across the road and entered the churchyard, which was spread out around the village church. The church was an old, wooden structure with clean lines and a bell tower that seemed to be part of the building instead of a dominant fixture, as some were.

This church was red—not white as most churches were usually painted—and this made Toby wonder, as he often had when he was a boy, if there was a reason for it. He aired the question out loud, and Roger, who knew the story, laughed.

"Yes! And a funny one it is. Many years back, like a century ago, the church was white. But due to its proximity to the fjord, it needed almost constant maintenance, in other words, re-painting. We have quite ferocious storms her, you know, and the church got plastered with sea-salt every time. Not good for the paint, nor the image. The paint was paid for collectively by the wealthy farmers of the village, but wealthy equals stingy, and when one of the farmers had had enough of this constant drain, he started to look for a solution.

"When he came across a large volume of red paint, meant for barns, he thought that he had struck gold, so to speak. He bought the whole batch and brought it home to Nordheim, and after he had had his barn painted—he had to get something out of it—he donated the rest to the church. The red paint was of course much more resilient than the white, and the results were less expenses for the farmers, an abundance of paint for the church, and a bright red church for all tourists to wonder about." They all laughed heartily at this as they turned the corner of said church.

Coming around the corner, they could see a man wandering around among the headstones in the churchyard, taking notes and photographs. He looked more than a little like the popular image of the slightly mad scientist, with his glasses a little askew on his nose, his hair flying in his eyes, and deeply immersed in what appeared to be some kind of research. Toby smiled a little at the image, but upon closer inspection, he found the man's wandering to be planned and structured, not as whimsical as it first appeared. He was also recording himself as he went along, documenting his efforts for later, further research, Toby assumed. On top of that, he was also apparently discussing the different angles of approach for his studies, as well as his findings, like how they could be interpreted, for example. They could hear this as they got closer, for his dialogue with himself was anything but silent and internal.

When he became aware of their presence, he straightened his back and beamed forth a wide smile to greet them. He had a pleasant face and a jolly twinkle in his eyes, as if constantly on the verge of breaking out in uproarious laughter. Physically, he was well-built, somewhere in his forties, with broad shoulders, a mop of brown hair, and the aforementioned glasses askew on his nose. With his contagious smile and his boyish appearance, he immediately caught their liking. What was there not to like?

The moment he opened his mouth, his American mid-west background was evident, but that did not detract from his charm. Quite the contrary. After introducing himself to them and shaking hands with them all, he stood there smiling.

"Now, what can I do for you?"

Instead of going through the whole background story, Toby cut straight to the core of the challenge they were faced with and started by briefly telling of their fresh encounter with Olaf's ghost. While he listened to Toby's story, Kenneth's eyebrows almost disappeared into his hairline and his eyes widened until his face seemed to consist only of two big, blue orbs. He was completely flabbergasted, and when he regained his voice, which had momentarily left him, there seemed to be no end to his astonishment, questions, and exclamations of initial shock and surprise. The trio just had to endure the flood stemming from Kenneth's amazement, until it began to dry out. When he had to catch his breath, Sandra seized the opportunity to start them over.

During the conversation that followed, they discovered that it was not so much what they had experienced that shocked him, but the fact that Olaf had been willing, even eager, to talk to them. That entities, souls and various kinds of immaterial beings did exist was something he did not doubt, given the evidence he had seen both first-hand and heard from trusted colleagues. What really surprised him, was that Olaf had sought them out. He explained that it was rare for newly deceased souls to make contact with the living, as they were disoriented at first, having passed into a new phase of existence. And in Olaf's case, to seek out his descendant and more or less continue their last conversation? But the piece of information that really got to him, was the message at the end of that morning's séance, the mysterious rhyme.

When he got over his initial shock, however, he proved to be a real asset in terms of knowledge and insight into Olaf's doings over the last two years, or the two last decades, more like it. It just happened to coincide with one of his own, deep interests, superstition or old beliefs as explanatory factors and tools in people's everyday life. When the thunder struck from the sky for example, what was it that made the thunder? Or the lightning? How was it that people could disappear on the fjord on a clear day? What made avalanches or rockslides happen? All of these things could, before the knowledge that science brought us, only be explained by divine or otherworldly intervention. But then their angles had differed, he said with another disarming smile.

Sandra confirmed that Olaf had been looking into these things, in fact they had worked together, but she did not think they had anything to do with Olaf's death. She told them that they had been looking at ancient practices and remnants of these in modern times.

Taking his que from her last remark, Roger piped up, "I hate to interrupt when wise people are talking, but if I don't get something to eat soon, I will become a remnant myself!"

Laughing heartily at this, they agreed that it might be true for more than one of them and moved over to the hotel to order lunch in the restaurant while at the same time continuing their conversation.

As they reached the hotel and turned the corner, Toby, who was bringing up the rear of the company, got a glimpse of a man in green, standing in one of the rose bushes. His initial thought was that it was a gardener, but when he thought about it, it was a strange thing for a gardener to do, to stand in the bush rather than in front of it. He turned back to ask the man about the rose bushes, he thought they were quite luscious and extraordinarily beautiful, but when he looked for the man, he seemed to have vanished. *Phew, that was quick!*

he thought to himself and turned to go into the hotel. He was as hungry as Roger, apparently having a mid-morning conversation with a ghost was good for building up an appetite, but he was a bit distracted on his way inside, something kept stinging his neck. Irritatingly enough, he did not seem to catch anything, no matter how many times he slapped himself on the back of his head, but fortunately, it stopped when he entered the hotel foyer.

The restaurant, they discovered, had a peculiar design that reminded them of, in Roger's words, "intertwining snakes." This was achieved with the use of many plants, dividing the restaurant into corridors and chambers, and so it offered very private nooks, where diners could sit in complete seclusion and enjoy their meals while talking without fear of being overheard, at least as long as they spoke relatively quietly.

As the room was nearly deserted at this time of day, they did not think it a problem anyway. When they sat down, the chat around the table quite naturally first centred around Kenneth as he was a new acquaintance to them all.

"I am what you call a paranormal researcher, or what most people would call a 'ghost hunter'" he began, as a response to Toby's questions about what he did professionally. "I have studied psychology, history, and partially archaeology, always with focus on the topic of religion, beliefs, supernatural creatures, and impact on societies. The last years I have been with the SOPHIA programme, at the University of Arizona, U.S.A. This last year I have also been a guest lecturer at the University of Edinburgh, working with the Koestler Parapsychology Unit."

"SOPHIA?" asked Toby. "I thought that was a robotics programme by…what's its name?"

Kenneth laughed. "You're thinking about that creepy android woman's head," he said, and shivered a little.

"No, if she'd been around, I would have been in the Arctic! The programme I work on is centred around investigating claims of communication processes involving deceased individuals, guides and/or angels, or higher powers or divinity. Healing and life-enhancement is what we look at, first and foremost, although my interest has always been the actual communication.

"But it was the job in Edinburg that brought me here in the first place; a lot of unfamiliar readings popped up on our monitors in the laboratories there. We measure ley-lines, amongst other things, and we suddenly got convergence readings that were way off the charts, emanating from this very spot, in Nordheim. So I came here, with all my gear, and set up measuring devices and recording devices to pick up any signs of this activity. That was a year or so ago. I have not picked up anything so far, but I have found a lot of interesting small divergences and a few people willing to be my sources. This was also the beginning of my friendship with Olaf, as he was the first person to sign up as an informant. I was given his name by the local librarian, who said that he was a veritable encyclopaedia, regarding ancient practices, mythology, and religion."

Sandra smiled at this; it sounded very much like the Olaf she had known.

"But does it not bother you that you haven't gotten any results yet?" Toby asked.

"No. In my line of work you have to accept that things happen when they happen, if they happen at all. The astral plane or whatever you want to call it, operates on its own schedule, and no-one can dictate it, not even a scientist!" he finished, still smiling. Toby could not help smiling back at him, his smile was contagious.

At this point, their food arrived, much to the gratification of Roger, whose stomach had been making itself audible for the last few minutes. They all dug in, though, for there was more than one hungry person among them if truth be told. It took a few minutes to still the wolf hunger before they were ready to go on, and Kenneth took up the thread of the conversation from where they had left off.

Now that he had introduced himself, he wanted to know who he was talking to, and they provided him with brief introductions, including a summary of their education. *It was almost as if they were applying for jobs,* Roger thought, *with quick résumés and CV's.* Roger and Toby, who were completely new to him, also supplied him with abbreviated versions of the info they had given each other the other night, and their characteristics of themselves brought a smile to Kenneth's face.

The other, relatively new, acquaintance to the other three, was Sandra, and now Toby and Roger, as well as Kenneth, got an insight into what she had been studying, together with Olaf.

It turned out that she was a witch. A real-life, practicing, and well-trained witch. At least, that was what she said of herself; not one of her three listeners had any experience with witchcraft, so they could not really tell.

"Ancient practices were what we were interested in, Olaf and I, and we had found quite a few extraordinary instances of this in the not so ancient past, as well as some really scary ones."

Kenneth looked at her thoughtfully at this, but did not ask any questions, he let Toby and Roger take care of that part. The questions came flying like snowballs, and Sandra had more than enough, trying to answer the barrage that the two were pelting at her.

"Sacrifice, real blood-sacrifice, was practiced up until the seventeenth century," she explained, "although, thankfully, we found no evidence of human sacrifice. Of course, that does not mean that it was not practiced, only that it was not talked about and therefore never recorded. Hence, no evidence could be found!"

Both of the young men looked wide eyed at her when she said this. "Blood sacrifice? To whom?" said Toby, but Sandra could not give him an answer this time. Olaf had not known, or were unwilling to share, his suspicions on the matter. The only thing he said, was that it did not appear to be worship of a deity, more a precaution taken to prevent something from happening.

When they had exhausted their inquisitiveness for the moment, it was Kenneth's turn, and now he wanted to know everything, every detail, however minor, from their séance that morning. After what felt like an hour's interrogation, although it only lasted fifteen minutes, when they had completely emptied out their memories and had nothing more to tell him, even if they wanted to, they fell silent, and so did he. He sat there, staring at his fingers, saying nothing, while they all looked expectantly at him, waiting for him to come up with some revelation, solution, or answer to their conundrum. At first, though, he was brooding over the things he had heard, but just as the three were beginning to itch with impatience, he began to talk, slowly and deliberately. It was clear that what he was saying was important, and to be absolutely sure that none of it could be misunderstood or misconstrued, he chose his words with utmost caution.

His first words were a question.

"Do you know how Olaf died?"

It stunned them completely, and Roger, to whom the question was directed, was taken aback by the direct stare that faced him. Uncertain as to how to answer that, he wet his lips, they suddenly seemed very dry, and started haltingly.

"I...I don't really know. The cause of death was attributed to a fall from great height, he was after all found underneath a cliff. Or, a sheer precipice, more like it. They thought that he had slipped, or maybe he had had a bout of dizziness or nausea. On the other hand, he could have tripped and missed his foothold. He was after all not a young man anymore..."

He fell silent for a minute, while the others looked intently at him. Then he finished his answer, almost whispering, "I received some photos from the scene of the accident, and I must say they scared me. I've never seen such a look of terror on a dead man's face...It must have been a scary fall!" This last sentence came very quietly, almost too low to hear.

The silence with which this was greeted was as heavy as lead, and Roger almost felt dizzy himself, trying to hold his breath in the tangible stillness that suddenly surrounded him. Then Kenneth, after studying him for a minute, broke the silence.

"I am not surprised. Unfortunately, for Olaf, he got too close to the core of the incidents he was looking into. I am convinced from what you told me, that Olaf's death was not an accident, it was murder, plain and simple."

The gasp that followed his statement, sounded like a strong gust of wind in the pine trees.

"What?" Sandra almost shrieked. Sensing that she was close to hysterics, Toby was quick to put an arm around her shoulders to try to calm her down, and eventually she did. "But who would do something like that?" she whispered.

"Yes, Olaf was a controversial person, and he rubbed some people the wrong way, but...Kill him? I do not believe it!" She then repeated the initial question, "who could do such a thing?!"

"Who? or what?" came the slow answer from Kenneth.

Staring open-mouthed at him, the three others blanched visibly at his statement, and in the silence that followed, their pulse thundering in their ears, the silence spoke more than a thousand words could have done.

Chapter 4

The atmosphere was explosive, to say the least, as all of them were staring at Kenneth as if they had just spotted a three-headed troll, or worse, a spectre. He, on the other hand, could feel his mouth starting to dry up as it always did before he had to deliver an important lecture, still he knew that all they wanted were answers, and he had just given them a lot more questions instead.

Kenneth knew that an explanation was not just needed, it was imperative, but he drank a glass of water before he began, just to moisten his mouth, while concluding his line of thought. Sandra looked at him, her eyes showing the emotions at work inside her. Hurt, confusion, and a considerable amount of apprehension were constantly flickering in them. Toby and Roger, who both felt steamrolled by now, by the events of the last 36 hours, were also apprehensive. That much was evident in their eyes. Then Kenneth began, and the tale that followed held their attention like no other tale they could remember. It was so improbable that it completely defied reason, and at the same time so honest and raw that it simply could not be a lie or a fake. Like the seasoned lecturer he was, Kenneth held them in suspense for some seconds before starting his story.

"Olaf had suspicions for years that something was off, not right, in this village or in its surroundings. When he first started wondering and asking himself questions about it, he initially thought that the many disappearances and deaths among the tourists were due to people going places where they were not used to go. People can easily lose their way in the mountains when they are on unfamiliar territory, and one wrong step may quickly lead to disaster, especially when the weather does not play by the rules. Which, of course, the weather never does, in some parts more than in others. Then, when he began to look closer at the phenomenon, he found that more villagers than tourists had been lost over the years, and the further back in history he went, the more ominous it got. Every year, since the records began, he found accounts of people vanishing or dying, both on the mountainsides and the fjord, and in unusually large numbers, but only one at a time, which in turn means that they happened relatively often. What struck him as odd, was the fact that the accidents or mishaps seemed to be concentrated around certain parts of the calendar year, with many incidents in a row, and then a longer pause before the next streak of events, so to speak. It was this that made him begin to suspect that something other than coincidence lay behind it, and he started to research the topic in earnest.

"His research brought to light the truly horrific numbers as well as some gruesome details about the many deaths. He found that the majority of the 'accidents' had taken place on what the locals called, 'The blacksmith's anvil'. A sheer cliff, a little overhanging, that dropped around hundred and fifty metres, or perhaps more, down into a gorge.

"Incidentally, that is where Olaf also met his untimely end. All the victims of that cliff, he read, was found with the same or similar look of absolute terror on their faces, their bodies plastered over the boulders down in the gorge. Not that these findings were something that could be read in a single manuscript, he had to do a lot of painstakingly slow reading in many different manuscripts, journals, and records before the picture started to emerge clearly before his eyes.

"After he had all these facts on the table, at least as many as he was able to search up—there were most likely many that he had missed or that had not been recorded, only whispered about—he started looking for connecting points, and to his surprise, he found several of these. One was that the deaths always took place on, or in the immediate vicinity of water, be it the fjord, a lake, a pond, or a stream or river. As an aside, there is a river coming down from the mountain top, right next to the Anvil, you know!

"Another was the fact that most of the incidents took place before sunrise or after sunset. Now you might not find that strange, as these hours are the ones when the light is at its murkiest, when the world is in the twilight zone, so to speak, but think; the majority of these incidents took place at a latitude and a time of the year when there is almost no night! Yet another was the little thing about the victims of the water, none of these were ever found, they vanished completely.

"In more recent times, the disappearances and accidents had spread out more over the year as ski-tourism increased, and several of the deaths were due to avalanches. Olaf always thought of these incidents as 'drowning in snow', and modern research has proven him right in that. And although most of the victims were found, not all of them were recovered, even with the use of SARs, or search and rescue dogs.

"But the number of people who were almost scared to death, was far greater than those who were killed. There were the many tourists, and not only tourists, coming back from mountain hikes and looking as if they had met a nightmare in broad daylight. Wide, staring eyes, sweat pearls on their foreheads, whey-faced, and shaky, they looked ready to plunge into the cold water and swim out the fjord, just to get away from the village, whatever might be in the water. Olaf tried to speak to some of them, but for the most part, all he got out of them was a whisper, 'Not alone…' and a slow, stiff shaking of the head. Some were a little more communicative, though, they spoke about a feeling of oppression, a gut feeling of panic, and an almost irresistible urge to run. Many of them gave in to this urge and were all out of breath when they reached the safety of the village. However, when Olaf tried to ask them about their experiences, or press them to talk a little further, they averted their eyes and they fell completely silent. The only tell-tale sign of their agony and bewilderment would be the veins in their foreheads, standing out and pulsing."

Kenneth then took a break to fill up his glass of water and emptied it in one swallow. Toby had a myriad of questions racing around in his brain, but his words got completely tied in a knot as soon as he attempted to phrase a sentence, so he decided to let them lie for the moment. Looking at Roger and Sandra he could tell that they felt the same way. Kenneth cleared his throat and excused himself, "I am used to lecturing, and one of the bad habits you quickly pick up, is to clear your throat all the time. It is very annoying to the listener and gives the lecturer a sore throat more than anything, but I am powerless to stop myself!"

The laughter that greeted this, was feeble and weak, but at least it was a laughter, they had all had their experiences with lecturers. He then resumed his tale, with the audience more captivated than any crowd he had ever addressed.

"Olaf began to suspect that all of these incidents, accidents, and mishaps were connected in more ways than just the water, so he went searching for the common denominator. Now, the beginning of this chain of events lay way back in time, and he could not find any records here in the village, so he went to the nearest town to research the library there, but without success. He ended up having to go to the national library over in Oslo to look in the oldest records they had, to eventually find a clue. It was written in the eldest rune-alphabet, a scribbled note on a piece of paper an archaeologist had left behind in a research file. It came from some ancient burial site that had been excavated in the mid-1850s, so it was hardly intelligible, and what made it worse, was that the runes were incomplete, torn out of context. But by then Olaf had a lot of information to fill in, as long as he did so with patience. It says something of the stamina and endurance he had!" Toby nodded. "I had almost forgotten that, but I suddenly remember a fishing trip where Olaf was adamant that we would not return without fish. The fish was slow to bite that day, and it got worse as the day went along, so we had all more or less lost hope. Except Olaf, that was, he kept going till nightfall, and what do you know? He came back home with the finest salmon I can remember ever having seen caught on a rod!"

"Anyway," Kenneth said, "after he returned, he had been convinced that the final answer could be found in the myths or folktales from this area, and as he already had a very good knowledge of these, it was easier for him to look up what he did not know from before than it would have been for you or me. It takes some knowledge to know what you do not know, if you know what I mean?" He was smiling as he said this, and they smiled back at him, relieved that the tension had been broken. When he continued, however, it was with a solemn look on his face.

"After researching everything he could, the theories that he had formed about what it was that lay behind the whole thing, had solidified, but as he told me; they were too improbable to be put into words yet. He set up some experiments instead, to try and flush out the culprit as it were, but he had no success during the first years. When I started up my research on the ley-lines, he became an informant for me, and gradually we became friends. He told me about his own research, and was of great value to my studies, because of his knowledge and his willingness to share it, but of even greater value as my friend, because of his ability to turn even the dullest or darkest moments into something we could learn from. He was truly a fine mind and a good man, and already I miss him greatly."

This last statement was greeted with some sniffling and discreet coughing as the trio around the table all took a leaf out of Kenneth's book and cleared their throats. Then he recommenced. "In my last meeting with Olaf, on my last visit before I went back to Britain, he told me that he had had what he called a breakthrough. He said that he had been in the pine forest high up in the mountainside, and then he had suddenly felt—more than heard—a chilling voice. Voice was the nearest he came to describe it, but it did not bear any resemblance to voices that he knew. It was in fact unlike anything he had ever heard before; a low, rumbling sound, harsh and malevolent, almost below the edge of what it was possible to hear, as if the earth itself was speaking. The voice—for lack of a better word—told him to cease and desist, or else his fate would be horrendous. Coupled with this, was the urgent feeling of having to escape, a rising, blind panic, and a growing sense of absolute horror. He said that he could feel his body slowly coating itself with a film of perspiration—sheer fear—and it was only by exercising a supreme effort of will that he was able to turn around and walk, not run, back the way he had come." He stopped for a second, then continued. "Olaf was still visibly shaken by this experience when I talked to him, but as determined as ever to see his objective through, now that he had finally made some headway. He was determined to find the answers that had been eluding him for so long. Three days after I saw him, I returned to the university in Scotland, and four days after that, Olaf was killed."

During the telling of this tale, his voice, which had started off in an almost conspiratorial fashion, had naturally grown louder, especially in the more dramatic parts, and the exclamations and outbursts from his listeners had done the same. This had caught the attention of a man sitting in solitude at a nearby table. He sat there, quite hidden behind a leafy plant, perhaps some kind of fern, huge and wide, and were now listening intently to what they were saying, his face reacting to every word. His name was John Peregrine, and like his namesake the peregrine falcon, he was always on the lookout for prey to appear. Being the village minister, that meant being vigilant regarding untoward influences or potential disruptors spreading loose talk and rumours around without any basis in truth, or to be more specific, the Bible. In short, anything that might have an influence on his parishioners' spiritual well-being, and this kind of talk was exactly the kind of thing that would get every one of his precious lambs worked-up and anxious.

Getting up from his chair, he had finished his meal and was leaving anyway, he made his way to the table of the company, and without any introduction at all, said, "I would keep that kind of balderdash to myself if I were you! My congregation has enough to worry about without your frantic superstitions plaguing them as well! Stupid youth, always looking for answers in the wrong and potentially dangerous places." He then turned his back on them, swinging his coat and umbrella so that he almost hit Toby, who was sitting closest, and marched off with one last, icy stare over his shoulder. Kenneth, who was used to this kind of abuse and reactions from the clergy, due to his line of work, just shook his head and sighed. The rest of the party found it exceedingly funny and was not in the least put off by it, in fact it was a comic relief after the serious and solemn story they had just heard and were trying to digest.

The intrusion of John Peregrine acted like a catalyst for the company, who now became less dumbstruck from the tale they had just heard and more action oriented, focused on what they could do to set the record straight. The breaking of the spell which they had been under, also made them realise that they were still hungry, and their food was lying on their platters, largely uneaten.

They now finished the rest of their meal, which was rapidly cooling, while they discussed what they had learned and, most importantly, what they needed to find more information about. Full at last, they got up and got ready to leave. Roger caught the attention of a waiter and asked for the bill, while the rest of the group tried to agree on how to go on from where they were. The one thing they immediately agreed on, was that giving up was not an option, even though Olaf's fate made going on seem slightly hazardous.

After some discussion back and forth, they decided on the different strategies they would use, most of which centred around the collection of information. Toby found himself wishing he could have known more about his grandfather's theories. That would have saved them some work now. But then he thought once more about it and concluded, "Then again, maybe not..."

The party then set out, making their way to the tasks they set for themselves that afternoon; Kenneth was going to the library for some research, and the rest were going to the pub. This could seem like an odd choice, but when it came down to information, the pub was certain to deliver, and on top of that, they needed a drink at that moment. As Roger said, "to heal our hearts and teach our woes to swim!" They all snickered at that, and then they went out in the sunlight and made their way to their different destinations.

When Sandra, Toby, and Roger arrived at the pub, they found it moderately crowded, but most of the people inside were buying beverages and snacks before going outside to sit in the sun. There were families as well as groups of teens, with the usual crowd of regulars thrown in for good measure. But since they were all sitting outside, this meant that there was more than enough room inside for them to sit down and chat in relative privacy.

When the men went to the bar to order drinks, Sandra gave them a warning, "I know that it is tempting to buy something strong to calm down your nerves after what we just heard, but it would be very unwise to do so. We need our minds in good working order, so let us keep to beer; that will help keep our thoughts straight if we moderate the intake!"

Toby and Roger both smiled at her choice of words, but they agreed with her on the issue, and bought three beers before looking around for a place to sit down. They once again chose a booth in the back of the establishment and took their seats.

Taking his first sip, Roger closed his eyes and sighed, "That one hit the spot! I can hear angels!"

Toby and Sandra laughed at that before mimicking Roger and sighing with intense pleasure. Silence fell over them as they gradually relaxed, but eventually, Toby started the conversation, "Wow! This has been quite a day, and it is not yet four o'clock in the afternoon! I wonder what's going to be next…" The laughter that followed this remark was definitely over the top and a bit hysterical at first, but eventually it acted as a catalyst. Tears of mirth ran down their cheeks, as they laughed at the situation, themselves and the other's faces, but eventually they got hold of themselves, and could relish the feeling as the last traces of tension left their bodies. When they had calmed completely down, or at least got themselves under control, they toasted each other's health and drank deeply while drying their cheeks. The few people who were inside the pub at that time, looked moderately bewildered and then shook their heads and went outside, laughing a bit overbearing. Not that the trio cared about that if they registered it at all.

Having caught their breath and collected themselves they were now in a state of mind where they felt that they could talk things over, and Roger opened the topic. Looking at them both with a questioning gaze, he simply asked, "So how do we proceed from here? We have learned that there is danger involved, and that we must be cautious, but what do we do?"

Toby looked at Sandra with a puzzled expression on his face—he had no clue at all—but fortunately Sandra had some suggestions. "As to 'what do we do', I have as little clue as you…That sounded like a bad song lyric! Let me start over." The men were laughing again at that, but they soon quieted down, and she gave it another shot, "I think that the best course of action is what we agreed upon, to do some research first. All of us, that is, not just Kenneth. To plunge into this without knowing somewhat of what we will be facing, could prove disastrous."

"I agree," said Toby. "Do you have any suggestions as to where we can find information?"

"Yes," came the answer, "I do. I will go to the library and talk to the librarian, Sissel, to see if I can track what Olaf was looking into and get a look at that. But we also need to talk to some people, there are folks out there that may possess vital information that they have no idea of, that might be interesting to us."

"Did you have anyone specific in mind?" Toby asked her.

"As a matter of fact, yes. The lady who runs the village grocery or all-in-one shop—it has everything you might need, and a few items you might want—is a very sharp but pleasant gal, and she is right in the hub of everything that happens in the village. Her name is Bridget Waters. She is a vital and young lady of seventy-something, with a superb memory of events, happenings, folktales, rumours, occurrences, and old-wife's tales. She will be a very good source to start with, I think."

"Anyone else?" This time it was Roger who asked.

"Well...how about your own grandmother? Belinda has a lot to tell you about the occurrences of the last century. I believe she took part in several search and rescue missions herself."

Roger looked a bit stunned at this piece of information, but nodded, "Ok, that will be a nice task for me, plus I get to visit my grandmother; it has been a while since I saw her!"

"OK," says Toby, "then I will deal with Bridget Waters. Who knows, I might learn something new!" He was smiling when he said that, though he was feeling a bit apprehensive. What would be the next thing to happen? "Anyone else?" he said aloud. "Hmm...I will have to think it over." Sandra answered. "You see, this village is very divided, due to the minister—whom we all have met—and his sway over the congregation. Also rumours and gossip travel faster than the speed of sound in this place, and people are generally wary of talking about things that are not strictly kosher, to put it that way. John Peregrine—that is his name—can turn into a quite nasty bump in the road if we do not watch our step! He was agitated when he left us in the restaurant..."

"Yeah," Roger chimed in, "he was livid when he left, and I know he has a bee in his bonnet about religion and ancient practises." "Like witchcraft, you mean?" said Sandra sweetly. "Oh, yeah! Definitely not one of his approved exercises! If he gets wind of what we are doing, or trying to do, he will quite simply blow up!"

"Then we will have to keep it a secret for as long as possible!" Toby concluded, smiling a little at the image of the minister going 'Kaboom!'

"What is the story with him anyway?" Toby asked, "I get a feeling he is one of those fire and brimstone-preachers, but he does not really look the part."

"I know," Roger replied. "He is somewhat of a conundrum, a crazed agitator for the extermination of witchcraft and ancient religions, a caring father to his flock, a model of puritanism, and a beguiling Casanova to all the single women in his congregation."

"Wow!" Sandra was genuinely impressed, "I had no idea. A troll of many heads, then!" This made Roger laugh so hard he nearly drowned in his beer, and Toby had to punch him in the back to prevent them from having to call the emergency service. In the end, Roger caught his breath again, and Toby and Sandra could give in to the giggles. Drying his tears, Roger continued, "He came to Nordheim about six-years ago when our former minister had gotten a new parish to care for. He created a stir from the moment he arrived, and one of the first people he met, was Olaf. They got off on the wrong tangent from the very beginning, and from there it just got progressively worse. Olaf could express his opinions in a very clear-cut manner, but the new guy was not much behind! They had some run-ins that are already the stuff of legend!"

"Oh, boy, I wish I had witnessed one of those!" Toby shook his head, laughing. "Yes," Sandra said, "but I think it is time we got back to business!" Smiling, they nodded their agreement.

While the three companions were making their plans and discussing their options, John Peregrine was sitting in his office. He had been furious when he left the hotel; angered by the rashness and what he perceived as stupidity in the youngsters. Well, to be fair, one member of the party was apparently an adult, but looks can be deceiving…Luckily, he had started to calm down the moment he entered the tranquilising environment of his church. Now he had regained his equilibrium, and was sitting in quiet contemplation, half listening to the lawn-mover in the churchyard on the outside; the church and its surroundings had to be kept in immaculate order, anything less would be an affront to his Lord! His thoughts were ever circling around the question, "What are these youths trying to do?" He was giving the problem deep consideration, as to go ahead without doing so could be hazardous, and he did not want that. In this, he was completely in agreement with the three companions, although for entirely different reasons. He pondered aloud, "Are they trying to raise the dead? Or are they trying to contact that which once was banished or wake what would be better left alone, asleep? Or could it be that they are looking for answers in all the wrong places, answers they would be happier and better off not getting?" Being a minister, he was fully aware of the dangers that lay outside our field of perception.

Dangers that could be roaming around us in our daily lives without anyone noticing until it was too late, and occasionally causing mischief or worse; downright destruction to happen! Brooding over these and more questions, he just remained sitting there in his comfortably worn chair, his eyes glazing over as he turned his mind inward to find the answers.

Chapter 5

Quite a few eyebrows had been raised during their stay at the pub, and if they had had a pound for each meaningful glance that had been exchanged, they would have been rather wealthy by the time they were wrapping up their discussion. Perhaps fortunately, the three companions were either oblivious to this, or they simply did not let it bother them.

Finishing their drinks, the three companions were by now getting ready to start their tasks in pursuit of their goal. "We need a name for this venture!" Roger suddenly said. "Now, let us see…The three musketeers…no, that has been used already. What about…" He went quiet for a minute while the other two were looking at him, half in amusement, half in excitement. "I know!" he suddenly exclaimed, "The Brazen Berserks! We are going to war against this…thing, after all! And if we look at what we are about to do, we could surely use a berserk or two." Laughing their way out of the pub, into the still hot sunshine, they stood there for a second before splitting up; Roger to first go see his grandmother, then to search through old family records, Sandra was heading for the library, and Toby was going in the direction of the village grocery shop. He had been informed that it was still open although it was by now five thirty in the afternoon. He was a little amazed at that at first, but then the barkeeper had informed him that the shop—as well as other businesses in Nordheim—was on 'tourist time', it opened in the morning at nine and stayed open until eight o'clock at night.

As they all turned around to leave, Toby noticed a flock of black birds sitting in what looked like an ash tree in a field across the road. The birds were quite big, much too large to be crows or magpies, and besides they were all completely black and shiny. But it was not only the birds that were huge, the tree also itself was a giant. He could not understand how he had missed it before, as it was prominent in the surroundings; it should have caught his attention the first time he passed it.

He looked at the tree and the birds in astonishment and wonder, and then called to his friends, "Have you ever seen such big, black birds before? Right there on the other side of the road, up in that huge ash tree? Do you know what kind of birds they are? Normally, I would have said crows, but I find they are much too large for that!" He was turning around when he said this, but he stopped when he saw his friends' puzzled expressions. "What do you mean, 'birds'?" asked Roger hesitantly, slowly making his way back to Toby. "I see no birds, nor any trees." He looked at Sandra for confirmation, and she shook her head, "Me neither."

"Seriously!" Toby exclaimed, "you cannot overlook them!" He turned back towards the scene across the road, meaning to point out to his befuddled friends what was right in front of their noses, but he almost lost his balance when he found that the tree and all the birds had gone, vanished into thin air.

Sandra, who noticed his stricken look, asked him softly, "Toby, were the birds huge and black?"

He could only nod.

"And the tree, did it seem to grow right into the sky?"

This time he had a little bit of voice, "Yes…"

She went and stood in front of him, holding him by the shoulders, "Toby, I think what you saw were Odin's ravens, and they were sitting in the branches of Yggdrasil, the world tree."

His eyes widened in shock as he digested this, "But…that is ancient mythology, stories and sagas! Was I dreaming? Daydreaming? Why?"

He was looking wildly at her for answers, and Sandra, who right there and then felt like a failed oracle, did not have anything to tell him, yet.

"I do not know," she said, and was about to tell him something more, but a wide-eyed Roger burst in with questions, a whole truckload of them. He had more questions than Sandra could begin to deal with, but she told them both that in her opinion, Toby's vision, if that was what it had been, was related to their quest, the only question was "How?"

"Perhaps we will understand it more when we have acquired more information and can get a more complete picture," Toby said, still shaky, reverting back to his academic language when he was distressed, looking for confirmation from the other two.

"Yes, I think you are probably right," Sandra replied.

Roger too nodded his agreement, "Well then, I am on my way to my grandmother, hopefully without any outsized birds attacking me on the way. See you at the library around eight?"

Sandra and Toby nodded and then they all left, going in their separate directions.

Walking the relatively short distance to the shop, Toby's mind was in total turmoil, as he was desperately trying to come to grips with what he had just seen, and how it pertained to the situation, to make some kind of sense of it all. But by the time he reached the steps to the shops he had concluded that he was failing miserably and resigned himself to what would probably be more of the same. *I guess this must be what it feels like to be caught in a tornado,* he thought, *or being sent over the edge of the Niagara Falls, stuck inside a washing machine, still going at full speed. Or perhaps sitting on a roller coaster, headed for a break in he rails and unable to get out, choking on the scream stuck in your throat...*Every time he was anywhere near equilibrium, he was sent sideways by something new. He shook his head and smiled a little at himself, relieved that he was still able to do that, and concluded that it was the best of his options right now, sitting down and bawling his eyes out was out of the question. Having finished his line of reasoning he opened the door and entered the shop.

When the door closed behind him, with a cheery tinkle from the bell, followed by a soft sighing sound, it felt like he was entering a cocoon, and he realised the equilibrium that had been escaping him these last days, was now waiting for him inside. The shop was empty and peacefully quiet, just the sound of a few flies buzzing around and being caught in the maze of goods on the shelves, the smell of coffee, and the soft clink of knitting needles at work. This last sound came from behind the counter, where the shop's owner was presiding over her knitting and—he could now see—a cup of coffee.

Putting what he hoped to be a reassuring smile on his face, he approached the counter and stopped right in front of her. She did not exactly look intimidating, but there was something about her, nonetheless. "Hello," he said, hoping not to startle her too much, but he was unprepared for the reaction he got.

Smiling back at him without lifting her face, she replied, "Well, I was wondering when you would turn up. You took your time getting here!" Taking a step back in surprise, Toby almost fell over when he collided with a basket full of yarn, but he managed to keep his balance and prevent the basket from emptying its contents, in the very last instant. Straightening up, he met her glance for the first time. She was scrutinising him closely with keen, grey eyes. The first thing he thought, was, *she does not wear spectacles* and the second, *she can see right through me!* Her face looked stern and intimidating, somehow, and this was starting to make him feel uncomfortable, but then she smiled again and spoke, "Hmmm…You look like Olaf, and yet not. More like Olaf would have looked if he had been born in this age and had the benefit of an education. Not that he was not educated. He was very well read and in addition, he knew many things that you will never find written in any books, if you take my meaning."

Toby was confused for a second or two; how on earth could she know? but then he relaxed; This was a small village, sour tongues would even call it a hamlet, and in small places there is always someone keeping tabs on people's comings and goings, who they were, and what business they had there and with whom. Her smile demanded an answer, and he found that the smile that now broke across his face was much more genuine than the previous. She seemed to pick up on that too, and her smile broadened. He then introduced himself, shaking her hand. She told him that her name was Bridget Waters and that she and Olaf had been very close. "He was very proud of you, young man," she said. "He would always refer to a telephone conversation or a letter for some anecdote or quote—A well-read and well-educated young man with his wits and heart in the right place and a healthy dose of humour, too—That was his opinion of you." She smiled a little wistfully. "He was so appreciative of everything you did, every time you called, every letter you sent. He would start reading those letters on his way home, nearly losing his footing on occasion, when you had told him something exciting."

"Could you tell me about my grandfather, please," he asked. "I have found a diary that he left behind, and it intrigued me so much that I would like to know more, if possible. Is it true that there are many tales from this area?"

"You can bet your sweet ass on that, young man!" Bridget replied, winking mischievously at him, and smiling again.

Toby almost reacted to that last remark with yet another step back, but instead he started laughing. It felt good, tremendously good, to hear his own laughter ringing free and echoing from the walls. Following Bridget, he entered the little space behind the counter and found that it led into a slightly larger place behind a wall. There Bridget had a perfect, secluded space, where she could sit, uninterrupted with her knitting, while keeping an eye on the door, on the lookout for customers. She invited Toby to sit down in a relatively comfortable chair and offered him a cup of coffee. "I keep the stronger stuff in my flat above the shop," she said, "so this will have to do for now. Besides, you need a clear head if you want to learn something new!" Sitting down and handing Toby his coffee cup, she looked him thoroughly over once again, at last concluding that, "Yes, you do indeed look like Olaf! You even have the same quirky smile that he got when he was a little embarrassed." Toby blushed a little at that, but as he had been told many times that his face was too honest for poker, he had no trouble believing her. Turning his thoughts back to the reason he was there he began his quest for answers. But first he had to ask one question, "Bridget, is it true that he was as stubborn as the talk says?" He had heard about this the night before, and was a little disturbed by it, because the stories he had been told, had not altogether been nice. "I would not call him stubborn," answered Bridget, "but I would say that he had a perseverance far beyond most people, or perhaps you could call it doggedness. This 'sisu' was what kept him going when other people would have given up, and brought him within arm's reach of the answers he sought. Unfortunately, it also brought him to his fatal end." At this, Toby's face went still, and he felt a tear trickling down his cheek. Absentmindedly, he brushed it away. "I thought so," he said quietly, "because of his diary. It was not the diary of a stubborn man, set in his ways, but a man driven by his search for the truth. And that can be dangerous because truth is a fleeting concept at the best of times."

"Whoa, now you are getting into deep waters!" Bridget was mildly impressed by Toby's way of expressing himself. Gathering his wits about him, Toby turned his face to Bridget, "And it is about his diary that I have come. You see, it is full of clues and riddles and half-finished paragraphs, and we urgently need some help to unlock the mind that has written it. In order to understand it fully, if you understand?" She nodded, "I will do my very best."

"So! What can you tell me, Bridget? Like I said, we are completely bewildered by some of the hints in his diary, and have very few clues to work with, so any information you can give me, is valuable!"

"Well," she replied, "I think it is best to start with the beginning, like Olaf always said, and in this case, it would—as you said yourself—be the topic of his research, the stories from this area. Some you may know already, and others will be a surprise to you, but anyway; here we go!" And then she embarked on a run of stories, fairy tales, and sagas from the surrounding area that left Toby wide-eyed, his eyebrows disappearing into his hairline.

She started with the tale of the ringing stone, that mysterious boulder way up in the mountainside to the south of the church. That stone was rumoured to be the entrance point to the fairy kingdom inside the mountain. It was a huge rock, lying on a ledge or shelf in the hillside, and it was said that when the church bells rang in the village, the stone turned three times counter clockwise on that shelf. The tale also went on to say that if someone were up there when this happened, they would disappear into the hidden kingdom and never return. That hidden kingdom was only ever seen by the unlucky—so people thought them—folks who entered it or were taken into it, and as a rule they never returned to tell what they saw. Nevertheless, the music of that kingdom could sometimes be heard; Bridget's own grandmother had had experiences with this. When she was a young child of around eight years old, she was sent up to the mountain 'seter'—a small farm of sorts high up in the mountainside where they would tend to the cattle and sheep during summer. Up there, with only the cows for company after the chores were tended to, that is the cows had been milked, and all the animals had been fed and given fresh water, then she would sometimes hear the fairies play music. The sound of otherworldly fiddles and strange singing would emanate from the very ground underneath her. All she wanted to do in those instances was to run down into the village again, but she had to stay put; the cows would need to be milked one more time before nightfall. So she sat there, often so scared she would cry a little, but she never saw anything.

The fairy that he heard the most about, was the 'hulder'; female, beautiful, and attractive beyond compare. She would enthral any man whom she met, and once he was completely under her spell, bring him into the mountain or cause him to get lost. Her male counterpart—'bergekongen', or the mountain king—was just as dangerous to the girls and women that met him. Those that did not fall for his enchantments were taken by force into the unknown. Many of the places where this was known to have happened, were still shunned, Bridget explained. But the fairies were not always wilful and dangerous, they could also co-exist and enjoy companionship with the humans. One place where this was evident, was the fairy dance place, an opening in the wood where the forest floor was flat with springy turf. It was located near to an embankment, on top of which was the dance area of the village; a wide, flat space.

Here, it was said, the fairies and the humans of the village would celebrate together on evenings like midsummer's eve, with dance and bonfires. They would see each other as shadows and hear each other's music like a ghostly echo.

Fairies were mischievous, though, and pranksters by nature Bridget told him, and they loved to play tricks on people. The instance with the cow on the rock was one of these. Once again it was her grandmother who played the lead part, she was herding the cows down from the mountain farm and made a short stop on the way to rest the animals and get a bite to eat. The cows were grazing peacefully next to an immense boulder that had come down as part of a rock slide many years ago. When they were ready to go on, she called the cows, but found that one of them—the nicest one with the most milk of course—was missing. She called and called, and she could hear the cow answering, but she could not see it. The irritating thing was that it sounded quite close, so she should be able to! Then she tilted her head back and looked up and behold; the cow was standing on top of the boulder next to where it had been grazing. That was not surprising in itself; cows can get onto many strange places if they are on the hunt for something good to eat, but in this case, it was an impossibility. No-one could have climbed up onto that boulder, especially not a cow. She ran home in a panic and got her father and three other strong men to come and help her, and in the end, they managed to get the cow down in one piece, but it took a lot of planning and wrangling (and quite the amount of swearing, although only after they had checked that no-one was listening in). Bridget's grandmother had sworn that she could still hear the fairy laughter from the surrounding woods even in her old age.

Listening to the stories gave Toby a sense of how life in those days, not that long ago, must have been. When he told Bridget this, she smiled, "Oh, yes, life was in many ways richer back then, even if the people were poorer, but at least they had a healthy respect for tings they did not quite understand." From there, she went on to explain about the mist you could sometimes see on the river, the frost smoke on the fjord and on the lakes, and the winter fog that would sometimes creep along the forest floor between the naked, black tree trunks. All of these were manifestations of elves, she told him, and one of the names—locally—for such phenomena was 'fairy-dance', the only visible sign of the fairies dancing, often under the light of the moon or the stars.

She kept him like that, nearly spellbound, eagerly absorbing every word, and at the same time thankful that he remembered to put his smartphone on 'record'. This was way too much to take in and remember. Then she went further, to several darker tales of horrible events, mysterious disappearances, and dramatic flights. These included chronicles of people dashing madly through the forest, barely making it to the village before collapsing, fainting dead with their eyes rolled back into their heads, showing only the whites. Toby listened as the cold fingers of dread crept along his spine. But what really shook him, was when he began to see a pattern; something sinister was lying at the root of these stories, and with a sudden jolt of fear he thought, *what if whatever this is, is on my trail at this moment?* Bridget was still talking when this thought hit him. Seeing his facial expression change from rapt attention to tense nervousness, she paused. She looked questioningly at him, her head a little tilted. When he spoke, his voice had a hesitant tone to it, "I hope it is only my overworked and taxed imagination, but did Olaf ever come here asking for stories, and if he did, was there any tales in particular he was interested in?"

"Yes…" Her voice was almost as hesitant as his, "there were indeed. He was very interested in all stories concerning the teeth in the water…" Toby just sat there—mouth wide open—for almost a minute, or so it felt. At last, Bridget spoke slowly; "I am guessing there is more to your request for local stories than you let on, but I will let you keep your secrets—for now, at least." Baffled, he looked at her, but she did not say anything more about that.

Suddenly, she was interrupted by the sound of the bell above the entrance door, and with an "Excuse me for a second!" she disappeared into the front behind the cash register. He heard a short and cheerful conversation—in German, no less—and then she re-appeared in the little nook. "That was a tourist, looking for a place where he could rent a boat for the day. I gave him the names and phone numbers to a couple of rental services, there are plenty of them around here. Although, when I think about it, I would never dare to embark on such a business in this place; Far too risky!" There seemed to be more to this statement than there appeared at first, so Toby waited patiently, while she settled down again in her chair. After sighing contentedly, pouring herself yet another cup of coffee, and taking a sip of the still almost boiling brew, she was ready to resume her story. However, when she went on with the tales of teeth in the water, her voice had subtly changed, and now it sounded more like…what? He could not make up his mind, but the thing she reminded him of was a bard or 'skald' as they were called in the old days. He sort of imagined that they would have sounded like her; strong, wise, and powerful.

The tale of the teeth in the water was a long one, and it had many stories woven into it; stories of shipwreck, sinkings, or ships and boats that had been trashed to pieces, as well as drownings or disappearances while swimming or bathing in the fjord, lakes, or ponds in the area. None of these seemed unnatural when taken one by one, but when they were considered together, a sinister picture began to emerge. As it turned out, no blood was ever spotted, no remnants ever found; all they could see was a big empty fjord or lake with no signs of life. Many of these incidents happened in an instant; one minute they could see a boat out on the water, the next minute it would have vanished without a trace. *Like ghosts,* Toby thought, *or spirits...* He was dragged out of his thoughts by the sudden stillness in the room. Bridget had stopped talking and was watching him intensely. He started to get up, fearing that he had made her uncomfortable in some way, but her next words brought him crashing down again in his chair, "Olaf always thought that the source of these accidents or mishaps was to be found in the mountains. He had even found the likely origin and was getting ready to tell me, but then he went and died..."

For a while they just sat there in silence, then Toby spoke up, "How can incidents relating to the fjord originate in the mountains?" He looked sceptically at her, shaking his head. "Think!" she replied. "Where does the water come from? Where do the sources lie?" Without answering, he turned around in silence and looked out of the window over the mountains, rising to the sky. Slowly, he nodded and turned back to face her again, "I see..." Once again, silence felt heavy on them, but this time it was broken by him turning off the recorder in his phone and rising from his chair, shaking his head to clear it. Bridget also rose from her chair and smiled warmly. He extended his hand, meaning to give her a handshake while he thanked her, but she walked right past his hand and gave him an almighty big hug. Blushing and grinning he hugged her back and thanked her a million times for all the help she had given him; he was really at a loss for words. Bridget, however, just tut-tutted and told him to come back anytime—even for shopping, as she said. Just then, the bell on the front door jangled, and a lady came into the shop. She was a middle-aged woman, perhaps near her retirement age, with a hawkish look on her sharp-edged face. Feeling her eyes on the back of his neck while exiting the shop, Toby was happy to be out in the open again, but Bridget's smile and warm welcome stayed with him throughout his walk to the library, the group's agreed rendezvous point. He was feeling elated, looking forward to seeing the others now that he had something to tell them!

On his way back through town, he noticed that although it was relatively late in the afternoon—one might even call it the evening—still families were gathering on benches along the quay, enjoying the warm sunlight and fragrant air. It was an altogether beautiful afternoon, without a hint of anything being amiss at all, and yet...he shuddered a little, feeling as if he had walked through a pocket of frigid air.

When he approached the rest of his group a few minutes later, however, everything remotely unpleasant was immediately forgotten. They were standing outside the library in a little patch of shade, talking and laughing. He felt warm inside, looking at them; amazing how fast you become friends when the circumstances are a bit out of the ordinary! He had puzzled over this on his walk, and he had concluded—at least temporarily—that as soon as the circumstances called for it, his accustomed patterns of cautiousness disappeared, and friendships were struck up, some of them to last, he hoped.

The group had met up outside the library as previously agreed, to find a place inside where they could sit down and compare notes, but as Roger remarked, the library seemed to be closing for the day. It turned out, however, that Sandra had an understanding with the librarian, Sissel Davik, as well as a key—something about studying for a bachelor's degree in social anthropology—and therefore they could take their seats and the time they needed in the now deserted halls. The four of them, after having had a standing chat about nothing at all, really, finally sat down for a discussion of their findings so far. After a quick discussion on the order in which they would go, Sandra started, telling them about her dive into the secret world of the library, and what it had yielded.

She had focused on the literature on folk tales and fairy tales, and as she said, "There is a whole plethora of different topics and creatures within this field. I would only have scratched the surface of the topic if I had not had some knowledge of it beforehand. Fortunately, I do, so I did some extensive digging in the field and found many interesting angles, but none that seemed to fit our present situation exactly. I also looked at myths from the area, thinking there might be some that could apply—like dwarves and fairies, for example—but, again, I did not find anything specific. Finally, I searched the Norse mythology and that is where I found the most promising leads. The tribe of the jotun, for example, 'giants' living in the mountains. A jotun is slyer than most, and much more intelligent than a troll, but I am not sure…I will keep them for consideration as we go along. There were some references to rock falls and disappearances anyway."

Next up was Kenneth, who turned out to have been doing much the same as Sandra, but from a different angle, namely the scientist's perspective. Where Sandra had been looking in books of history, folk studies, and social anthropology, he was looking into research on the topic of "insubstantial beings and their influence on the fabric of reality as perceived by humans." In short, supernatural entities messing with human lives. The two angles of investigation seemed to run in parallel lines, though, and much of the same beings or entities were included, but there the two approaches diverged. In Kenneth's world, it was all about energies, there was no evil, good, bad, benign, destructive, or constructive. Energy could have results that could be perceived as good or bad by humans, but there was no intention behind it, it struck out haphazardly in certain locations, all based on the conditions that were prevalent there. This was—of course—completely at odds with Sandra's views, and she was clear on what she thought about it. "Energies?!" she exclaimed disbelievingly. "You would chalk off all these incidents to energies striking out haphazardly? Excuse me, but I am not buying that!"

"So you would rather imagine beings of some extradimensional version or other, doling out their punishment or approval after some sort of internal—and highly illogical—logic?! Because that would make so much more sense!" Kenneth's tone was not just a little bit sarcastic when he answered.

This sparked a discussion, where she and Kenneth had very strong, opposing views. Kenneth, who proved to be a clear advocate for atheism, argued that anyone who tried to exonerate him or herself from the consequences of their actions by using the unseen level as an excuse was stuck in the dark ages. Sandra, on the other hand, was an advocate for multiple planes of existence, the one we exist in being one of these, and all inhabitants of these different planes have their own agendas and reasons for doing what they do. Kenneth scoffed at this, although that view was also held by a fair number of his science colleagues. He obviously had no regard for their line of reasoning and kept saying that he had hitherto had a view of Sandra as an intelligent person, but that he might have to reconsider this. He had a smile on his lips while he spoke, though, so that the edge of what he was saying was not very sharp. Sandra did not seem to mind his wording either, so it was evident—after a short pause where both Toby and Roger held their breaths—that Sandra and Kenneth were merely continuing a discussion that had long since began and which had never been ended. Toby and Roger just sat there, listening wide-eyed as the discussion went back and forth. They did not understand it all, especially not Roger, who had landed in this without any prior knowledge. Except childhood fairy tales, of course. Toby, after all, had had some introduction through his studies, but still he found it a tough chore to follow the discussion. In the end, without them reaching a conclusion, Sandra was the one to call a truce, "Let us just agree to disagree, shall we? I have a feeling that what we are looking for may end up giving us the answer to our discussion." Kenneth smilingly agreed to this, with Toby and Roger clearly showing their relief and agreement, and so they went on to Roger and his search in family history and legends.

As it turned out, his grandmother had had quite a few stories for him, more than he expected. Of course, there had been the normal, well-known ones—fairy tales and myths from the area—but there were also tales that he had never heard before. "It was a revelation," he told them. "Some of these tales belong to the 'unspoken knowledge'—things that everyone knows but no-one talks about." She had told him about the fear that the anglers harboured regarding the treacherous fjord and its mysterious disappearances. Whether they were fishing alone or in groups, the thought of what might happen to them lay as a haunting spectacle over their heads.

She had also told him that the reason they called it "the teeth in the water," was a young child—a boy—who was out in a small boat with his father, fishing and just enjoying himself. While he was looking down into the depths, trying to see the bottom, he suddenly asked his father "Dad, are there wolves in the fjord? Cause I can see an awfully big mouth with lots and lots of teeth!" Laughing, his father had turned around to answer, only to find the boy gone without a trace. No trace of him was ever found, even though they searched for almost two months. His father killed himself three months later, leaving his wife—seven months pregnant—to care for their two-year-old daughter. When he heard this, Toby jerked a little, making Kenneth look at him for a second, but when Toby did not say anything, he looked back at Roger.

That story left them all shuddering as a chilling silence descended. It was Roger who broke the silence at last, "I don't know about you, but this is beginning to give me the creeps, or should I say, beginning to escalate the pressure." Kenneth coughed and cleared his throat before he gave an answer, "Clearly, there is more to this than I suspected, and I suggest that when we go forward in this investigation, we do so with caution. Whether you believe in beings from other dimensions or scientific explanations, you all have to agree that this is uncanny as well as highly unsettling." They all nodded in agreement.

Toby then took the floor, relating the stories that Bridget had told him. Amid the many raised eyebrows, 'Oohs', and

'Aahs', he more felt than saw Sandra's attention rise and her blue-green eyes watching him intently. She was intensely interested in what he could tell, and especially when he got to the last stories, the ones about the teeth in the water. When he started on them, he looked at Roger for a second, and noticed the facial expression and his mouth forming a surprised "Oh!" Just like with Roger's tale, these stories left an unpleasant, chilling silence in the room, and this time it was Kenneth who broke it. "There it is again! But this time we have a direction for our investigation; the mountains!"

"Yes," said Sandra, "and if I may suggest a starting point, I think we should start with the cliff where so many have lost their lives, last of all, Olaf."

Toby nodded slowly, then said in a low voice, "I think so too, but Kenneth is right. We have to be cautious and wary, there is something behind this and I doubt if it is going to just let us look at things without starting some sort of trouble." The group sat there, looking at each other.

After a long silence where every one of them sat lost in his or her own thoughts, they started up the discussion again, but this time it was directed towards practical concerns. These included what equipment would be needed for their investigative expedition, what security measures they would need, and, not least, when they should start. Fortunately, Kenneth was well equipped in connection with his research, so all the necessary measuring devices were to be found in his rooms. The struggle would be to bring them up to where the actual researching would take place. As for the question of when to start, there were some radical suggestions, like midnight or the dog watch, but they finally decided on eight o'clock in the morning. Other things that were up for discussion, was how they should prepare for it, what was wise to eat before such an adventure, how they should be dressed. Roger put forward the idea that they should all be dressed up as goldfish to confuse their toothy opposition. This was greeted with a hearty laughter from the group, leaving them feeling a lot less tense and more relaxed.

In the end, they had discussed all that they could think of, and as they ventured into the night and felt the warm air surrounding them with a pleasant scent on the breeze, they could feel the excitement about the next morning and what they were going to attempt. Roger and Kenneth spent a few minutes waiting for Toby and Sandra who were putting the chairs back in order before they left the library. Alone in the dimming room, Sandra noticed a look of thoughtfulness on Toby's face. "What is up, Toby?" she asked softly. "What is on your mind? Is there something more you think we should have covered?"

"No," he said, then he looked at her, "or yes. There is something that won't let go."

"What is that, then?" He stared into the gloom. "Just…The look on Olaf's face when he faded away." This left a deep stillness in the room, and quietly they finished putting up the chairs before joining the other two on the outside. As each went quietly home to their own lodgings, Roger and Toby made their way back to Roger's house where they sat down in the living room. Roger opened a bottle of fine whisky and filled two glasses with the amber liquid.

Sitting there, in his cosy living room with a drop of high-quality spirits in their glasses, their chatter turned invariably, perhaps inevitably, to the topic that occupied most of their waking minds, and probably their subconscious as well. They talked through the course of action they had agreed upon earlier, featuring Kenneth with all his instruments as the nave on which their whole plan hung. They were going to go up the mountainside towards the cliff which Olaf fell from, registering every fluctuation in the readings once they got up there. "Good thing Sandra went along with this," said Roger, "I was a bit worried that we would have another discussion between her and Kenneth!"

"Nah," answered Toby, "she is way too smart for that. I kind of like her, you know." He added this last bit almost as an afterthought, and Roger smiled, almost imperceptibly at that. They chatted on, now more lightly, and got a warm, mellow feeling as the minutes ticked by. The evening wore on, and in the end they both got up and started up the stairs, bidding each other good night. Nevertheless, when they lay in their beds, both men found themselves submerged in their own thoughts and with a curious, feeling of anticipation in their stomachs.

Sandra, having gone back to her temporary accommodations in a lodging house almost in the centre of town, was tired. But she was too excited for sleep to come, at least yet. The events of the day, the intense and joyful moments, the wonder, the frightening stories, the comradeship with her two new acquaintances, they all joined forces to keep sleep at bay. As if this was not enough, she was also deeply worried, although that was a thought, she kept to herself. In fact, she did not even want to admit to or think of that feeling of anxiety, but it was undeniable and persistent. Sighing, she brought out her tarot cards and picked a card at random. When she turned it over, she got very close to screaming out loud, which would have woken her landlord. It was Death, grinning toward her from the face of the card. She quickly put the cards back in the box where they used to reside, and drank her tea hurriedly, thoughts racing. The card could mean anything, a change of direction, a fresh start, the splitting of a friendship, there were many possibilities. But somehow, she knew that this time, it carried ill tidings for someone, someone she knew. Sleep did not find her for a long time.

In a house near the church, Mrs Charlotte Reignan, a widow in her early sixties, was enjoying her evening cup of tea while gazing out of the window, looking at nothing in particular. She was thinking about the day and the events it had held. First, there had been a committee meeting at Mrs Thornson's. Amelia was the perfect hostess, serving tea and coffee, and those nice sandwiches with salmon—absolutely delicious! And the cakes... *I am glad I am naturally thin* she thought to herself, then smiled a little. Those cakes were so good, they were positively sinful to eat, but she reckoned it was a minor sin, and, besides, the cakes put them all in a splendid mood for talking and planning the next half year of activities in the church club. After their deliberations were ended, she had gone for a march along the shore on her way back home. That would have been great, too, if it had not been for all the youngsters, running around, splashing in the water, and making noise. She detested noise and unruly behaviour, always had. Her late husband had liked the little monsters and the sound they produced, he thought of it as 'the sound of life'. Well, he was long gone, having died suddenly at the relatively young age of 55, and she would not have to pretend to agree anymore. On anything. Not that she had really ever done that, only in public to avoid losing face in the eyes of her peers.

Thoughtful now, she put her cup down and allowed herself to be absorbed in daydreams. Or to be exact, THE daydream, the one about herself being swept away by the man, the authoritarian, yet tender hearted man of her life. She sighed softly, then slowly opened her eyes and smiled gently to herself. Anyone who knew her, would have gasped had they seen it, because that was a facial expression, they did not associate with Mrs Reignan. While finishing her tea, she thought about the new boy, Olaf Larsson's heir. He looked nice enough, but looks may be deceiving, and in this case, they were more than likely to hide a misled or misleading person, one that could be dangerous to the young in the village. He was a person she definitely would have to talk to Mr Peregrine about. He would know what to do, she was certain of that.

Getting up, she went to the kitchen, rinsed her cup out under the tap and put it into the sink. Walking up the stairs to the bathroom on the first floor, she was humming a tune to herself, searching for the words to go with it. The lyrics came to her as she entered into the master bedroom *Onward, Christian soldiers!* She felt it immediately; it was the perfect song under the circumstances, telling the world that the good Christian soldiers of the parish would not budge in the face of opposition or subversive forces, they would stand straight and look their adversaries in the eyes!

She was still humming and smiling when she drifted off to sleep twenty minutes later.

Sophie and three of her best friends had stopped by the pub that afternoon, arriving just as the three self-proclaimed investigators were leaving. She looked after Roger, whom she knew, and wondered who the other two were, but then she was drawn into the conversation with her friends and forgot about the trio. She had a wonderful time, enjoying a good meal and beverages in good company. The only thing that bothered her, was a feeling of being stung in the neck by small insects. She tried to swat them with her hand, but just like Toby—if she had known him—she kept coming up empty-handed. Her girlfriends' reaction when she told them what was bothering her, was to laugh and make light of it, but one of them said, half-jokingly, "You are being watched, my dear! Look out for a dark stranger!" When they went on with their recounting of the latest village gossip, Sophie took a time-out and looked behind her to see if there was someone looking at her from behind, but no-one was to be seen, only groves of trees, thickening into a forest a little up in the hillside. Shrugging her shoulders, she turned her attention back to the talk around the table and forgot about the whole thing.

Chapter 6

In the early hours of the morning, somewhere around half past five, Roger opened his eyes and sat up in bed. Cocking his head to one side, he sat there listening for several minutes. Something had woken him up, a noise or sound of some sort or other. When he did not hear any more, he got out of bed, put on a pair of jeans, and went downstairs and into the kitchen. Looking out of the window he saw another brilliant day, sunny and warm even though it was now barely six o'clock and the day had not even started properly. By clock standards, anyway. What nature thought of the concept of 'standard time' and 'daylight saving' was unknown to him. He snickered a little at that. He could hear Toby beginning to move around up in the guest room, and so he put on the coffee before doing anything else. While waiting for the coffee to brew and Toby to come down, he went out onto the porch just to 'smell the day' as he used to phrase it. He was standing there, his face to the sun, when he suddenly heard the music again, the same music, he suddenly realised, that had woken him in the first place.

It sounded like nothing he had ever heard before and it seemed to come from the ground under his feet, or was it from the rocks? He could hear some sort of stringed instrument playing an eerie melody of sorts while accompanied by flutes, drums, and deep ringing tones. Although eerie...He had learned about Schoenberg and his dodecaphony at school—funny what you remember—and this had a strong likeness to that, interspersed with oriental sounding phrases. As for the deep, ringing, bell-like sounds; "Tubular bells?" he wondered. He suddenly remembered the story about Bridget's grandmother, and he realised that if she had heard something as weird and—sinister? Was that the right word? If so, it was no wonder she had been scared out of her mind.

He was still standing there, listening intently, when Toby came out on the porch, and joined him, bringing with him two cups—or mugs—of coffee. They took their seats in the chairs and sat there in silence, just relaxing, for a few minutes. Or silence; the music was still playing, varying in intensity and decibel, but always present. The only thing Roger was not sure of, was whether the music was 'real'—in other words audible—or if it was just 'in his head'. He studied Toby's face closely, and from what he could see from the expression on his face and the look in his eyes, he knew that Toby was also hearing something. Relieved, he looked down into his cup for a moment, searching for answers there, but then he plucked up his courage and asked him straight out, "Toby, you look like there is something on your mind. Could it be that you are hearing something unusual, new or strange?"

Toby looked shocked but decidedly relieved when he answered, "Yes! I am hearing this weird, outlandish music—have been hearing it since it woke me up this morning—and it is still playing. Do you mean that you hear it too?"

"Yes," Roger answered, "it woke me up as well in the wee hours of the morning and have been giving me a most unusual feeling—half anxiety and half trance-like—all morning. I can hear some sort of outlandish string instrument, flutes, and drums, and I am wondering if there could be tubular bells as well. There are some deep, ringing tones that have to be a large instrument at least."

"So do you only hear instrumental music?" Toby asked. "Yes," Roger answered, looking inquiringly at him. "Do you hear anything else?" he asked.

"I hear choirs," Toby said. Roger looked at him, wide-eyed.

"There are two choirs, and they are very different from one another; one with reedy, sylph-like voices, sweet and soothing, almost dreamy, and one deep and rumbling, almost harsh and hard, a male choir. If choir is the right word, it seems more like one voice split into many—an organ—one voice sounding like a multitude of voices all being ominous and forbidding. At least as far as the male choir goes, the female is more like a girls' ensemble, but with a much bigger range than normal voices." Roger's forehead filled with furrows, "You mean one male and one female choir? And with vastly different content and message? It sounds almost like two opposing forces at play here, but how do you see these in the scheme of things? What do you think they mean? You know, if I had not been a part in this, I would have called that a fantastic scheme for a movie soundtrack…Except it is not." The questions came tumbling out in a flood, and Toby had barely time to draw his breath between them. "Whoa!" he exclaimed, "not so fast! You must give me time to answer one before you fire off another! Besides, I do not have any idea of what to make of them. I—or we—will have to discuss it with Sandra and Kenneth before we land on any ideas. Perhaps we will need to get more information, observations, and facts before we can begin to agree on an answer." The music that they discussed had faded away while they talked, and now only the sunshine, the sound of insects, and the birdsong remained. They both got up—another sound had entered the morning: rumbling stomachs—and went into the kitchen to get some much-needed breakfast. Roger cooked bacon and eggs, a solid start on what they anticipated would be an eventful day, considering what they were about to embark on.

A little past eight they met up with the other two members of their party outside the library. Standing in front of the building, surrounded by rucksacks with equipment, Sandra and Kenneth looked like they were still having a discussion. *She looks awfully sweet when she is caught up in the heat of the argument,* Toby thought then blushed. Roger, who was busy thinking about what they were up to, did not notice. Sandra, discussing lively with Kenneth, found herself looking at the cousins approaching them. They were quite similar in build and quite handsome together, but Toby was by far the most boyishly good-looking of them she thought—quite out of context—and then she felt a warm surge electrify her body for just a second. Totally taken by surprise, she lost the thread of the discussion for a moment and looked around at Kenneth, only to find him scrutinising her with a twinkle in his eyes. Lifting his eyebrows until they resembled a question mark, he just smiled at her, which made her blush and fluster. Toby and Roger, coming up to them, greeted them with a "Good morning!" in near perfect chorus, and Sandra and Kenneth responded with a "Morning!" in return.

Before they got down to distributing all the equipment between them and doling out tasks, Roger and Toby told

Sandra and Kenneth about the music in the morning hours. They both looked nonplussed at first, not really knowing what to say, as they had not had any similar experiences. However, when Toby talked about the two widely different choirs he had heard, he thought he saw a glimmer of recognition in Sandra's eyes, but she did not say anything. *Perhaps she was not certain,* Toby thought, *or it could be that she—for some reason of her own—was withholding her judgement for now.* After Toby and Roger had told them their story, Kenneth stood there without saying anything for a minute. When he spoke, he was totally professional, "Okay, it sounds like we have more than one conundrum to deal with. The best way to tackle them is one at a time, and time is running." His words acted as a catalyst that got them going again, so they put the question of the music and choirs off until later and got back on track with the task at hand. First, they finished off distributing the rucksacks with equipment between them, making sure that everyone got what he or she could handle. The purpose of this expedition was after all to find out more about the oddities, not to check the participants individual strength and stamina. Secondly, with the rucksacks packed, the straps adjusted, and everything in order, they set out on their expedition, following the path through the wood and up into the mountainside. All of them regarded themselves as reasonably fit and able to handle the workloads they took upon themselves, but nevertheless, they were all out of breath and sweating freely by the time they reached the first clearing on their way up the mountainside.

Back in the village their departure had gone almost, but not quite, unnoticed. One pair of eyes had followed their preparations on the outside of the library and continued to observe them until they disappeared into the forest. Of course, it was a way of life in the village—observing your neighbours and other people passing by—and in the same way, it was an accepted pastime in a certain segment of the population to gossip, speculate, and to pass judgement on the actions of everyone from the smallest child to the eldest inhabitant. 'They should have known better!'

These eyes belonged to just such a person, considered by some to be the backbone of the village society, and by others to be the worst gossip and slanderer the village had ever known. Adding to that was a mean disposition and a 'better-than-thou' attitude that left no room for human consideration. She even looked the part. Hair in a tight bun on the back of her head, steel-rimmed glasses, thin as a rake, with sharp edges; she looked like you could cut yourself on her if you got too close. Though Mrs Reignan would not have recognised that description of herself. In her mind, she was righteous, strong, and concerned with the well-being of every individual in the village of Nordheim. If she could be seen as sharp, that would be because she knew the old saying "Spare the rod and spoil the child" had the ring of truth to it. She would never have let the youngsters of this village get away with what others—less vigilant people—called pranks. She was always the one to call it for what it was, devilry! And, of course, she was slim. Gluttony had never been a vice in her! If Toby had cast a glance back over his shoulder, he would have recognised her as the customer in Bridget's shop as he left it the day before. Out for her morning march—not walk, that would have been too pleasant and soft—she stood in the shadow of a hedge and watched—or spied at—them. When they disappeared into the forest, and were lost from view, she stepped forward and turned to go home. This would need some thinking and she did that best over a cup of coffee in her own kitchen. Her eyes narrowed to slits and her brows furrowed as she started to march back.

That morning, Sofie Oldnes, contrary to everything she was known for, had almost thrown a temper tantrum. This was due to the extreme un-cooperative and downright infuriatingly stubborn attitude of her cattle. They refused to go out from their boxes, they refused to let her attach the machine so they could be milked, and when she finally got them to go into the milking booth, they had all mysteriously gone dry. She had spent more than twice the normal time on the mornings chores and was still nowhere near finished. "What is the matter with you?!?" she asked in exasperation, as she pushed the last cow back into its box. The cow did not answer that, she did not really expect it to either, it was more of a 'ask the question or scream in frustration' kind of thing, but then the cow turned its head and looked at her. She nearly tripped as she took a step backwards. The look in the cow's eyes was one of pure fear, a terrified facial expression that shocked Sofie so much, she also found she had dropped the bucket of bread she had been holding. Turning slowly around, she took a good look at her cattle, and found identical expressions were visible on all their faces. They were terrified, she realised, and for a moment she found herself wishing they could speak. Then she stopped herself, did she really want to know? Shuddering, suddenly feeling sick to her stomach, she ran out of the shed and into the house, wanting to cry, not knowing why. Behind her, the cows watched her run without a single sound, the silence was absolute.

They had only just begun their little expedition, but already they were feeling winded, or wrung out, due to the heat of the day. It was scorching hot, and it was only eight forty-five. "Half an hour!" Toby could be heard muttering, "Just half an hour, and I feel like I've been running a marathon! Or perhaps a triathlon…So much for a cool summer in the north! This feels more like a sauna than a summer if you ask me." His grumbling made Kenneth laugh, "I know how you feel. I felt the same way when I came here the first time, and I believe I complained a bit about it. Quite extensively in fact! But Olaf just smiled at me and replied that if I gave it some thought I would realise why the summers in Norway could be so intense. And of course, he was right. The short summers in Norway are the payback for the long, dark, and seemingly unending, miserable winters that anyone living here will have to endure. It is no wonder their summers have to be intense." Toby had been busy drying his sweat while Kenneth spoke, but now he smiled ruefully and reluctantly nodded his head in agreement. "Sure, I understand that, but normally I would be sitting at an outdoor restaurant at this point, and heat feels somehow different when you have a fan over your head and something cold in your glass!" At that, they all laughed, before drying their sweat and continuing with measured steps in slow motion.

After about half an hour's further walk, they reached a plateau—or sort of; it was more a less steep hillside—where they decided to rest for a while. The walk had been strenuous for all—Toby's complaining aside—and the breather was more than welcome. Toby was the first person to sit down and take his flask out of his backpack, meaning to empty it into his mouth, and the others were following his example. Only

Roger remained standing, and he broke the thirsty silence before they could start drinking.

"Nice and easy does it! Do not empty your flasks in one gulp unless you really want a headache or a queasy stomach."

They all looked up at him, and Sandra asked the question that was in the eyes of them all, "Why? Why should we be careful? It is only water! And by the way, why aren't you sitting down and resting? Isn't that what this break was for?"

"Well, if I wanted to get all stiff and sore, I would have sat down. As it is, I prefer my muscles in good working order. And considering the water, yes, it is only water, but drinking—or gulping it down—when you are as hot and sweaty as you are now, will only lead to 'brain-freeze'. A very uncomfortable feeling which is usually accompanied by a hefty headache. The best way to refresh yourselves when you go on a strenuous hike, is to immerse your hands or feet in running cold water—a brook or small river will do. That way you cool down your blood faster and more efficiently than by merely sweating, and you can avoid the 'disasters' that can arise from overheating and drinking too fast." As Roger spoke, the rest of the company was sitting there, looking decidedly sheepish, but the moment he finished, they all scrambled to get first to the small brook that was joyously playing among the pine trees. Kenneth was in such a hurry, Roger had to remind him to take his shoes off first. It did not take long before the air was filled with sounds of contentment, and it was a much fitter company that set out for the last leg of their mountain climb.

It took them about twenty more minutes of hard walking to reach their destination, but when they did, it was all worth it. They found themselves on a shelf in the steep mountainside, and when they turned around, and beheld the view that was laid before them, their eyes widened in wonder. The dramatic landscape, with forest, thundering waterfalls, nooks, and crannies, unfolded before them, nearly stopping their breath. They could also see the village far below as it lay there beside the fjord. The fjord itself glittered in the sunshine as if it were filled with gemstones. *It reminds me of an animal, a ferocious and wild one, at rest. Like a deep blue-green dinosaur—a carnivore—peaceful and lazy for the moment* Toby thought to himself. He also noticed that you could follow the stream from the glacier river far into the fjord, as it was a hazy whitish, green colour from the sediments it carried. Sandra suddenly spoke up, "Olaf used to call it 'the sleeping dragon' because it looks as if it has a coat studded with gems, and it can wake up and wreak havoc quicker than a tornado when stirred!" Toby nodded slowly, "I can see what he meant, beautiful, but deadly!" Kenneth then called for a group talk before their adventure would begin, one which included food and drink, and a sit-down. This was greeted with a sigh of relief from the rest of the little company.

This time when they sat down, all being properly refreshed and having stretched their legs and backs, they were looking forward to a bite to eat and half an hour of relaxation. The walk up to the clifftop was strenuous on the best of days, and with untold kilos of equipment in their backpacks, it had been exhausting. While they ate, they discussed their plan and how they could best move forward in the safest way, weighing the different approaches against each other, trying to decide where to start. If the whole group went up together and set up shop up there on the shelf by the steep mountainside, they would feel a lot safer, but as Kenneth pointed out, they would also miss out on a lot of data collection, as the action was not going to be registered in just one spot. This was a point they all recognised, and although there was some discussion on this, they relatively quickly agreed to Kenneth's suggestion, as he had the experience and skills needed in this kind of experiments. The rest of their break was spent just chatting and enjoying the sunshine. There was not a single speck of cloud in the sky, birds were singing everywhere, and the day was just plain gorgeous now that they did not have any heavy hauling ahead of them.

Finishing their break, they got to their feet and brushed off their behinds. There was a lot of good-humoured laughter at Roger's attempts to brush off Sandra's fanny, which kept being out of reach. Suddenly, she stopped and tilted her head, "Listen!" she said. All four of them stopped what they were doing and turned their attention to the sounds they expected to hear, the sounds that had been there just seconds ago. And what they heard was nothing, nothing at all, no birds, no brook, no soft whispering in the trees, just emptiness. Alerted and somewhat on edge, they suddenly noticed an almost inaudible sound emanating from the rocky terrain. This sound, if it was a sound at all, did not resemble anything they had heard before, and it lasted only a few seconds but left them all feeling skittish and uneasy. Kenneth remarked, half-jokingly, that it reminded him of the warning signs of an earthquake. This was not greeted with the mirth he had hoped for, and smiling feebly, he excused himself. The sound did not re-occur, however, and after a few more seconds the normal sounds of birds, other wildlife, and the little brook, returned and gradually made them relax, but not completely. They did not quite go back to the mood they had been in. All of them found themselves more aware of any change in the soundscape, however minute, but as the minutes went by and nothing kept happening, they focused more on their tasks and less on their surroundings.

Kenneth was perhaps the most focused of them all, since he was after all used to being in a scientific mode while in a laboratory, where he would be required to keep an intense focus on the experiment or proceedings taking place, something he excelled at. This was a very good quality in a scientist while in a laboratory, but in the field the drawback was that this made him totally oblivious to other things that were going on around him. So he did not notice the shadow gliding across the grass in his direction. It was just a small shadow, seemingly cast by a small, quick, and agile animal, but it grew as it drew nearer, taking on a menacing quality. Sandra, who had been pre-occupied with an un-cooperative piece of machinery, suddenly looked up sharply as if alerted by something. Noticing the shadow, now racing towards Kenneth, she raised the alarm with a shout, "Hey!" The reaction of the shadow entity was nothing short of terrifying. It immediately started to spin violently in a retrograde motion, like a mini tornado, creating a whirlwind that threw Kenneth off his feet and then slammed him to the ground. Some pieces of his equipment had been picked up by the wind as well, and was now threatening to drop, or perhaps being thrown, on his head. Fortunately—or perhaps intentionally—the equipment pieces thudded down next to him. Then, as suddenly as it started, everything was normal, once again.

Toby and Roger, all shook up by what they had just witnessed, ran to Kenneth, and knelt beside him, shaking him, and calling his name. He came to, quite bewildered, and confused, but quickly regained his wits. The others were frankly quite shocked by his vigour and energy once he had re-established his foothold, "I knew it! We are onto something, and it's clearly much, much bigger, and vastly more intricate than we even suspected! Wow! My colleagues are going to be completely flabbergasted!" Toby smiled back at him, uncertainly, "Eh, you don't want to give up and get down while you can? I mean, it seems sort of dangerous, or perhaps malicious is a better word.

"Plus, I can't really see any one of us being able to control it, and to be honest, right now we are shaking in our boots, all of us!" Kenneth, who had bent down and was intent on reassembling his gear, now looked up. Looking around, staring all of them straight in the eyes, he said in a voice so low it was almost a snarl, "I do not give up! Not in this life and not in any next existence if there is such a thing. I am determined to find out where the root of these occurrences lies, and if there is something with a mind or intelligent design who is behind it all. For Olaf's sake, because I owe it to him, and for science's sake, because this clearly needs to be documented and solved, if possible." Raising his voice to almost an opera singer's decibel, he called out, "Do you hear me? I will find you and I will lay your secrets bare, that is a challenge!" He looked wildly at them all in turn without saying another word, and then he resumed what he had been doing when the mini tornado appeared. Glancing around at the other two, Toby saw that their eyes had the same mixture of uneasiness and determination that he himself felt, but at the same time communicating without words that they too had made up their minds to go on with the expedition. No words were needed, they all set about their tasks with renewed energy and a kind of reinforced resolve.

After twenty minutes of hard work, assembling machinery, hooking up laptops and synchronising strange gadgets, they were ready to start. Kenneth, who had initially been treating this expedition as a kind of exiting adventure, was realising that it was indeed an adventure, yes, but a very dangerous one. So he was now controlling, and testing, his equipment for the third time, determined that it would not miss a thing.

He was worried—this was way bigger than he thought it would be—but he was also resolved that they—he—would solve the mysteries and find a logical explanation to what lay behind it all. That, however, did not stop him from turning his slightly pale face towards Sandra, asking her if she would or could provide some form of shielding for them while they performed the experiment.

"Not that I really believe that they work, but if there is some…something intelligent behind this, maybe it believes? It is just to have all our bases covered if you know?"

Nodding slowly while taking in his expression, she replied, "Okay, I will see what I can do."

Problem is she thought to herself, I don't know what we are up against. All I know is that it is powerful, immensely powerful, and angry.

That being said, she started laying out her paraphernalia, choosing what was needed, and taking the utmost care with the placing and directing of each part. While she was thus occupied, they all became aware of music. It drifted towards them, seemingly coming from the rocks themselves, sounding like eerie pieces of strange origin, played on outlandish, yet somehow familiar, instruments. As Roger and Toby had told them about the music, they had heard that early morning, the sound was not unexpected, but unsettling, nonetheless. Wasting no time, she soon had everyone adorned with amulets that were designed to protect them from ill will or intent. They all accepted these without comment, even Kenneth, and watched as she hurried back to finish her protection of the area. When she turned and faced them, she had a warning for them all, "These amulets will protect you, but they only hold so much power to repel attackers. If the attack is stronger than the amulet…well, it will not be of much help, I'm sorry to say."

"Have you ever come across something like this?" Roger asked her. "No." came the answer, "I have never encountered anything nearly as powerful as this, and I can tell you one more thing; We've only witnessed the beginning!" The three men looked at each other, then, in silence, they set up the remainder of their equipment, and the experiment could start. They got ready to take up their positions without saying anything, all the time conscious of the music, barely audible, but ever present.

Chapter 7

The first order of business when they started up, was for all four of them to sync their diverse equipment with Kenneth's main laptop. It was going to monitor, control, and record every reading from each of their gadgets, so it was important that they got it right the first time. When the quartet had all finished these initial procedures, they gathered yet again for a brief talk before starting the next stage of the experiment. Kenneth was serious when he addressed them, and very direct in his remarks, "Okay, this is different from what I expected. It is going to be more tense than I foresaw, and it will likely be quite dangerous. So if anyone has any doubts, now is the time. I will not think ill of you if you decide to go down to relative quiet in the village instead of going through with this." Toby, Roger, and Sandra exchanged looks, then shook their heads. "In for a penny, in for a pound," said Roger. "Besides," chirped Sandra in, "we couldn't leave you alone up here. You'd get befuddled and wander off for sure!" That remark set off a bout of laughter, nervous at first, but then relieved.

Feeling much better, as they always did after a healthy laughter had released the tension, they started to take their positions. As they did so, they all suddenly noticed that the barely audible music had now gone completely quiet. None of them commented on this, but they all looked slightly puzzled, nonetheless.

Roger and Toby, each of them equipped with several gadgets with lights, switches, and dials, were going to be the 'field agents', going up to the rock face where the mountain rose steeply into the sky. Sandra would remain in the clearing with Kenneth, going around the outer perimeter there and constantly checking the readings. She was already completely immersed in the job when the two of them left.

They set out through the wood in the direction of the mountainside. The instruments they were carrying were constructed to measure different aspects of the background radiation or energies, as well as the electromagnetic and the ultraviolet spectre, plus any sounds in the wider range, the one inaudible to humans.

The instruments all seemed rather outlandish to Roger, but to Toby they made sense, being instruments of science. *At least, they could give some unbiased answers to what was causing this,* he thought.

When they reached the mountain wall, rising straight up from the ledge of sorts they were standing on, they first put their equipment down and stretched their backs. Standing there, they took time to admire the scenery before starting up properly. *It was spectacular*, Toby thought, and for a moment the feeling of loss that was brought by it and the memories this evoked, nearly made him choke.

As they turned around to get their gear and get into position, they suddenly noticed a great slab of rock, almost perfectly round, fitting into the mountainside like a door. Toby and Roger looked at it, curious but cautious.

Toby stepped forward and knocked, making a flippant remark about how he should check if any hobbits were home, but Roger was more restrictive in touching it, "Careful, Toby," he said, "don't go ringing the doorbell when you don't know who might answer."

They both started to laugh, but stopped abruptly, both of them leaning forward to take a closer look. On the outside of the circular stone, a fine line of scratch marks could be seen, but they seemed...intentional?

"Do you know what this is?" Toby asked, with awe in his voice.

"No," said Roger, "but I am sure you will tell me when you have figured it out!"

Toby looked at him, then back to the markings, "It's runes," he said, "old runes...I wish I had paid more attention when we had this in my studies!" Fishing out his phone he took pictures of them, hoping to unlock the mystery later, in peace and quiet.

Now, at last, they were ready to start. They first took up their positions about 100 metres apart and turned to face the forest and the view. Straightening himself up, Toby looked at his measuring devices and lifted his eyebrows in surprise; there was not a single reading on any of them! "Hey, Roger," he said into the microphone, "is there something wrong with your equipment? Because mine seems to have died!"

"Well, actually, I thought I had made a mistake with the calibration of mine," Roger replied, "because it does not seem to be functioning at all." Then Kenneth broke in, "Guys, this is totally unheard of. I have never gotten readouts like these on any of my instruments before. There is always something to register, background noise if you will, but now they all seem to have gone comatose—all dead, not receiving—while at the same time we have been witnessing and hearing so many strange things with our eyes and ears it could fill volumes! They seem totally devoid of input—any input—and that is, as I already told you, an impossibility. It is almost as if there is a conscious mind behind this force, trying to shield itself from detection." The last part of the sentence was difficult to hear, as he started muttering to himself, tapping the screens and dials with his index finger, and shaking his head. Toby and Roger stood where they were, nonplussed, as they listened to him checking and re-checking the machinery and computer hooked up to his instruments, not finding anything wrong with either. Apart from the missing input, that was. Then he suddenly chimed in again, "I wonder if you could walk around the area a little, to see if I can find out what is wrong with these damned pieces of machinery or see if I can at least pinpoint what the problem is. If that is possible…" He faded out again, but Roger and Toby started to move around as he had instructed them, and before long, the dials on their gadgets started to register…something.

At first, it was merely an odd 'blip' or two, and then the steady, humdrum 'noise' re-emerged. But among that noise, which was supposed to be there, some strange spikes appeared on and off, and then…it started to get decidedly strange, very strange indeed. The dials started turning first this way and then the other, waving like hands in a parade. Then they started spinning, first slow, then faster and faster. Toby dropped his metre in confusion and not a little fear, but he picked it up again, only to be greeted with all the colours of the spectrum, flashing in front of his eyes. Back in the clearing, Kenneth was watching the progress of his two investigators up on the narrow plateau. He was gasping and staring with wide open and bulging eyes—anyone coming up there and seeing him like this would either have called the emergency services, or they would have thought him raving mad and turned tail and run for their lives—as the spikes and waves showed up on his displays, some of them way off the computer's registering capabilities. He did notice, however, that the spikes and the general levels of registering seemed to be at its most intense whenever one of the sensors approached a certain spot in the mountain wall. Standing up and grabbing the portable version of the registering device which he shoved into his backpack, he started marching across the field to go and investigate it closer. As he started walking, he contacted Toby and Roger on the walkie, directing them towards a rendezvous point a little way up in the mountainside from where he was currently standing.

Now, you might think that walking on a mountain is a relatively easy task since it has basically two directions, up and down. But as anyone who has ever tried to walk in unfamiliar mountain terrain can tell you, it can be very bewildering and misleading, and that was what Kenneth now found out. It did not take him long to get lost. The undergrowth was thick and unyielding in places, and so he veered off course. *Not much,* he thought, *getting lost in a mountainside is not easy, there are always two directions that can be easily detected, namely up and down.* Snickering a little at his own wit, he stopped to catch his breath and get his bearings. He also contacted Toby and Roger on the walkie-talkie, explaining that he was a little lost, but that he would still join them in the not-too-distant future! He could hear them smiling as he let go of the 'Talk' button. Turning to his

GPS and turning on the screen, he was fully expecting to see his position somewhere in the vicinity of the mountain plateau, but when the screen with the familiar dot appeared, it did not show the mountainside at all!

His eyes were blinking much like the screen he was looking at, as it showed his position in the middle of the North Sea, a little west of Doggerbank. Before he could process this, the GPS blinked again, and now he was on the North Pole! Well, not exactly on the North Pole, he seemed to be 50 miles or so to the west of the actual pole, but still...He was utterly confused, and kept shaking his head at the weird behaviour of the device as it planted him in Siberia within a few feet of the banks of the Kotuy River and just a few miles from where that river runs through the town of Kresty. He was shaking his head and knocking on the display with the finger knuckles of his right hand, to see if that helped somehow, but no; the display just kept on showing him popping up in the most outlandish places on the globe. "It's a good thing this piece of crap doesn't have other planets in its archives!" he grumbled. He was so completely absorbed in what he was looking at, that he failed to notice what was happening around him.

A sound had crept up on him, seeming to come from everywhere at the same time. It had been below hearing range at first, but now it was getting so loud and high-pitched that even a preoccupied scientist simply had to notice it. It was the sound of music, but a music so eerie and wild, in fact almost alien, that it really defied description.

Flutes, drums, harps, strings, harsh brass and wailing woodwinds, all in a cacophony of noise, and under it all, the voices that Toby had heard that morning. High and quavering, low and menacing, harsh and brutal, soft, and sorrowful, they all blended in a mix of terror and desperation. Kenneth felt like the breath had been sucked out of him, and all he wanted was to lay down, cover his ears, and scream along with the music. He dropped all the stuff he had been carrying down on the ground and shielded his ears with both hands, but to no avail, he could still hear it. It permeated everything and seemed to come from inside his skull as well as from the rocks, the plants, and the sky. He was bending over, slowly sinking to the ground, when he perceived a voice at the very bottom of the music. A voice so low it was felt more than heard, like the rumblings of a mountain about to erupt. It was filled with a rage and a fury so cold, so intense, so overpowering, it rendered him frozen, chilling his bones and blacking out his mind. A horrendously strong gust of wind suddenly struck out of nowhere, caught him where he stood, hunched down, lifted him clean off the ground and threw him over the edge of the cliff. So completely frozen by the violent emotions was he, that he was unable to even scream until suddenly, when the ground disappeared below him, his vocal cords were freed from the restraints that had been on them, and he screamed wildly, agonisingly, as he plummeted to his death, several hundred feet below.

Up in the mountainside across the fjord, opposite from where the expedition was taking place, Sofie Oldnes was out looking for the cattle she had there, preparing to serve them some treats in the summer heat. She was carrying a plastic bucket full of pellets—yummies for cows—and had regained much of her ordinarily good mood, when she heard the scream coming through the air, followed by echoes. It entered her brain like a bullet, making her lose her grip on the bucket as she clasped her head and covered her ears. Tears were welling from her eyes and her body was shuddering, shaking like a leaf in the wind, as she stood there crouched, listening to the dying man's desperation. She could feel herself losing consciousness, slipping to the ground, and her only thought was, *I can't take this anymore, I'm leaving!*

In the clearing where they had made their base, Sandra had been totally immersed in her job of watching the dials and screens, as well as keeping an eye on her protective amulets and warning system. She was writing down an observation with a couple of questions when suddenly she felt sick, horribly sick, to her stomach. She whipped around and let it go into the bushes behind her, almost projectile vomiting and nearly hitting a squirrel that was hiding in there. The squirrel, looking very annoyed, even vexed, turned his back and disappeared into the trees. Slowly, she straightened up and used a handkerchief to wipe her mouth and face. Her stomach felt instantly better, now that it had discharged whatever it was that had upset it, but she still felt a little queasy. Or perhaps uneasy? She looked around and listened intently, no, not a whisper of anything unusual or strange, but still she had that little lump in her stomach. Standing there for a moment, she decided to sit back down again, but she turned towards Kenneth to let him know that she was okay. He might not have noticed anything at all, as immersed as he was in his studies, but then again, he might surprise her. When she could not see him anywhere, she just stood there, nonplussed. Wrinkling her brow, she looked around the clearing for him, but he had disappeared completely. *Now where has he got to?* she thought to herself, then realising that he had probably gone up to Toby and Roger, due to the problems they had earlier, she lowered herself back onto her seat, smiling a little, only to spring back to her feet a couple of seconds later.

A whirlwind—a perfect funnel—had appeared on the edge of the clearing. It was spinning mind-blowingly fast, and was edging closer to her, inch by inch. She took a stance, straightening her back, squaring her shoulders, and holding her hands out in front of her, spreading the fingers like fans, as wide as she could make them go.

Chanting one of the ancient spells she had practiced with Olaf, and visualising herself in a blue bubble, she watched the funnel die out as suddenly as it had appeared. As she lowered her defences—slowly and cautiously—she heard a scream, or perhaps there were two, echoing around the mountain walls. It was a desperate sound, a scream in mortal fear, bringing the adrenalin rushing back into her system, preparing her for whatever was in store, as she began to dash up the mountainside to where Toby and Roger had gone. She never stopped to think, the urgency in that scream held all the information she needed to bring her into action as she sprinted towards the sound.

On the ledge by the mountain wall, she found Toby kneeling beside Roger, who appeared to be unconscious. For a wild moment, she looked up into the sky, just to see if anything there could have hit him on the head, but then she shook it off and turned towards Toby, "Has he fallen?!?" she asked, terrified that Roger might have tried some stunt and paid the price for it. "No," came the answer, "but he saw something.

"Or maybe he heard something. Anyway, what he experienced scared him so badly that he fainted—shut down."

"Where is Kenneth? He should definitely know about this!" Sandra was upset, and that queasy feeling was back again, together with a feeling of imminent and deadly danger. "I saw that he had left the clearing, was it to come up to you?" She looked into Toby's eyes, imploringly. "We haven't seen him, but he was on his way, that's true," Toby answered. "He was on the walkie to say that he had lost his way for a moment, but that he would be here soon." Sandra felt terror creep up her spine at those words, and her certainty grew, something terrible had happened. She scanned the forest behind and beneath her with an almost pleading intensity, but nothing could be seen. Kenneth had a good sense of hearing, so he should have heard the terrifying screams a little while ago, unless he had fainted, of course. The thought that he could be the source of those screams was promptly pushed to the back of her mind, but it was there, nonetheless. She straightened her back and turned back towards Toby, who was looking questioningly at her. "We will have to go down in the forest and search for Kenneth," she said, "he might have fainted or worse, so we better find him quickly." Toby nodded his agreement and stood up in silence.

Together, they got Roger up on Toby's shoulders, and they began their way back to the clearing with Sandra supporting Roger while Toby shakily made his way down the hillside. When they got down into the forest of conifers, they spotted Kenneth's walkie lying on the ground there with other pieces of his equipment lying scattered around it. Sandra stood there, still as a statue, while Toby gently eased Roger down and sat him against the leg of a huge pine tree. Looking at each other without a word, Toby and Sandra then turned towards the cliff and slowly made their way towards it, walking as if in a trance. As they came closer to the cliff's edge, they started to slow down, almost reluctant to arrive, but helpless to stop their progress. Moments later they were standing on the edge, looking down. Because of the shadows—or it could be the film of tears in their eyes—it was difficult at first to see what was down below, after all it was three hundred feet down there—at least, but there was no mistaking the image anyway. In the ravine at the bottom, they could make out Kenneth's backpack—looking strangely like a piece of doll equipment—and next to it, like a discarded and badly used toy, lay the body of Kenneth, still and broken. They just stood there, comforting each other without words, tears rolling down their cheeks.

They walked slowly and in silence back to where Roger sat, still out cold, both of them totally empty and drained in body and mind. As they reached him, they looked for signs of re-animation, but there was nothing, not yet anyway. Taking out their cell phones, they tried to get a signal, but much like Roger, they were out of reach and temporarily 'dead'. The camp was only a little way away, so they made their way back there, walking slowly and without much talking. To an uninformed or unsuspecting bystander, they would have appeared like zombies, with vacant expressions and empty eyes. It seemed as if someone had just pulled the plug that supplied their energy, or perhaps their energy was being drained away by that same unseen force that had so brutally killed Kenneth? They gathered all the different gadgets and devices together in an ordered pile, before picking out what they could carry. After that, they set about waking Roger up, a task that proved gargantuan, but at last they were successful. As anxious as they were to see if there had been any harm done to him, they still sat back and studied him closely. *Is he still in there, or has something else moved in?* Sandra thought while a cold thrill ran down her body. When he opened his eyes, he seemed confused and disconnected, but then his eyes cleared, and his mouth opened as if he was going to scream. Toby hurriedly put his hand softly against Roger's lips and said with a quiet, mild voice, "It is okay, there is nothing to be afraid of now. Shhh!" Still Roger looked around him in the manner of a man who had seen the devil, and Toby felt close to panicking again.

Roger—when he came properly to—was shocked at what they had experienced, but mostly he was aghast at what had happened to Kenneth. Silent tears streamed down his cheeks as they related the story, at least as much as they thought they knew. "Remember," Sandra said, "we do not know for sure what happened, but I am convinced that the force we are up against, saw Kenneth as the most dangerous adversary, and decided to deal with him first when he did not want to back down."

"Yes..." said Roger. "If only we had gone to meet him instead of waiting up on the plateau! Perhaps, if we had come down to meet him, we could have hindered the force or entity or whatever the f...you want to call it, from killing him! I saw it! That's why I fainted. A huge shadow came straight out of the mountain, through the door we found!" He was looking at Toby when he said that, then he looked down as if it was painful to go on. That shadow had the shape of a gigantic man, and it had eyes! They were glowing, red and menacing! When it looked at me, I fainted clean, maybe I even screamed, "I don't know...But we might have been able to save him, somehow!"

"Or we could be dead along with him." Toby was looking down when he said that, but then he looked Roger straight in the eyes. "There are a lot of ifs and whats and could-have-beens in this, and nothing we say or speculate about will make us any the wiser. Except for giving ourselves bad consciences, without any grounds or reason for it."

At that, they all stood up in silence—there really was not anything more to say—and began their descent through the forest. Roger was still a little uncoordinated due to his shock, but he got progressively better as they moved down the mountainside. When they reached the spot where the reception on their cell phones came back, Toby called the police and informed them of the accident that had taken place. As the police had offices in the next town, it would take them about 40 minutes to reach the village by speedboat, and even longer to reach the clearing and the plateau, so it was agreed that the three survivors would meet them at the library where there was room for them to sit and talk, before they started the process of retrieving the body and the equipment. After he hung up, they all sought each other's faces with their eyes before looking down again. Quietly, they resumed their descent while the sun—a deep red hue now that the day had passed, and it was getting on towards the evening—was colouring the mountain peaks in front of and behind them.

Chapter 8

They reached the library before the sun went behind the mountain, being greeted by Sissel who had had a telephone from the police before they arrived. She ushered them into the library and made sure their backpacks and equipment were safely stored.

Then she found them a conference room where they settled down. When she learned what had happened, she was very helpful and efficient, while at the same time deeply worried over their well-being. She made coffee, tea, and even rustled up some scones for them. *Some people think anything can be fixed when you only have a full stomach!* Toby thought sadly. Then he smiled inwardly at himself just a little, feeling that they might be onto something after all. But then his eyes clouded over with a fresh film of tears again, and he realised that this would take a long time to recover from. *Time and patience,* he thought. Then another thought jolted fear back into his system. *What if that power, that destructive, angry, malevolent power, still had it in for them? What if it was coming for him next? Or Sandra? Or Roger?* The mere thought of this caused his body to be coated with cold sweat, making him shiver in spite of the temperature outside.

The police arrived around fifteen minutes after that, and they wasted no time in setting out, after they had checked the three survivors. A psychologist who was part of the municipality's crisis team, stayed with Sandra and Roger, while Toby walked with the police back up to the spot where it all happened. First, he showed them the clearing with the equipment, and then he took them to the cliff where they could see for themselves the remains down in the ravine. One of the officers, a boulder of a man who had been standing in the background, laid a hand on Toby's shoulder and conveyed his condolences, for which Toby was grateful. *I can't believe I did not notice this man on the way up here!* He thought. But then the situation and reality came back to him again. It occurred to him that his—and the other's—relationship with Kenneth had grown both strong and deep despite its short duration. He was glad for one thing, what had happened that day had left no marks or signs of any kind on the landscape, and so it was likely to be seen as another accident in the mountains. Kenneth was known to be somewhat of an easily distracted professor type, and so he could—at least in the opinion of many in the village—be prone to walking straight into thin air when preoccupied with a problem.

Down there, far below them, he could see small lights moving slowly but steadily upward. The rescue, or retrieval, team could be seen making their way through the ravine on their way to get the body and get it back to the village. Toby could also hear a helicopter in the distance, so he guessed that they were being picked up as soon as the body was secured. As he stood there on the edge, feeling the loss of his new friend like a heavy lead ball in his guts, and with tears leaking silently from his eyes, he was surprised by the unexpected friendliness of one of the police officers, the aforementioned boulder. Axel Hoegh was his name, and as 'hoeg' means tall in Norwegian, you could say he looked the part. Well over two metres tall, he came over to Toby and gave him the biggest bear hug ever, while saying softly, "I am sorry for your loss, lad. Very sorry." Toby allowed himself to be comforted like this for a little while, and when the hug ended, and they were ready to go back down, now laden with the gear that he and his friends had used the morning carrying up, he felt strangely better. Adding to his relief, was the fact that there had not been a single little sign of anything untoward. Neither sounds, strange happenings, nor sights had presented themselves to the new spectators. And when he thought about it, that was probably just as well. They would not have been able to handle it, he thought, or, rather more precisely, his head would simply have refused to deal with anything more.

When they arrived back down in the village, they were just in time to witness Kenneth Barker's body being placed inside a mortuary car for the transport to the morgue. *It must have come with the ferry,* Toby thought, a little disjointedly. Roger and Sandra were standing by the side of the car, saying their quiet farewells as it slowly turned onto the road and began its journey. All three of them then followed the police officers into the library and sat down for a formal interview. It took a while, two hours at least, or maybe a little more, but then the officers thanked them, gave each of them a card with the name and phone number to a psychologist, and bid them farewell—for now. There might be more questions for them later, but it looked like a straightforward case, death by accident. After they got all the necessary contact information, the police left, leaving Toby, Sandra, and Roger, feeling strangely lost and alone.

Standing there, in the shadow outside the library building and feeling like the discarded debris from a road accident, they slowly became aware of the many askance glances from the crowd that had gathered there on the other side of the road. This crowd had started to come together when the mortuary car first parked outside the building. Others, who joined the crowd somewhat later, had followed the movements of the police once they became aware that something was afoot and had watched from a distance as they brought down the body of the scientist. Now the people in this crowd were busy comparing notes, discussing theories, and coming to conclusions.

Most of these were wildly inaccurate, based on hearsay, beliefs, and personal likes and dislikes—gossip in other words—and not meant for anything other than spite or slander. In Nordheim, as in many other small villages, this was a form of entertainment, however dark, acting both as an affirmation of the beliefs and prejudices held by a certain portion of the villagers and as ostracism of the outsiders. The outsiders were of course Toby and Sandra, with Roger thrown in for the purpose of an example; look what happens if you take up with strangers! Most of the stories that were created cast the three friends as the villains, and their offenses ran from neglecting to help when the scientist was caught in a delusion, or went into a frenzy, or ran from a spectre, or was simply lost, and to them being actively involved in his demise by pushing him over the edge! And why?

Jealousy, perhaps, or arguments, who knows? Because you cannot really tell, can you, with strangers?

Sandra, who was very sensitive to these vibes from the crowd in front of them, told her two friends that they should leave before the it got ugly and started to yell at them. Nodding in agreement, they decided to leave, but where to? In the end, they decided to carry all the equipment back to Roger's house, and sit down there, as that was the most private space they could think of. They all felt the need for space to breathe, time to think, and the opportunity to mull over what had happened, as well as consider their options and what to do next. Since they expected the media to come running in droves, once they got wind of what had happened, this was their window of escape, so they better not waste any time. They gathered up the instruments and devices that were standing there on the sidewalk, put it in their backpacks and started down the road through the centre of town. Fortunately, there was a lot less of these gadgets than there had been when they started out this morning, because the police had taken the majority of Kenneth's equipment with them to a laboratory to see what they had registered, or to check them for signs of foul play, perhaps? Toby did not know, and right now he did not care. As they made their shuffling, slow way down the main street—the only street—he only noticed the people standing in groups, averting their eyes when the three passed them, and joining heads and whispering as soon as they had passed. He wanted to scream, "Yes, we are sorry! Yes, we have lost a good friend due to something we do not understand No, there was nothing we could do!" but the words dried out on the way out of his mouth.

On their way down the street, walking slowly, or rather shuffling, they all noticed the expressions on the faces on both sides, and to their surprise, they found that quite a few of them were sad, sympathetic, or commiserating. They were actually beginning to feel a tad better, when the figure of a woman came marching up the street, approaching them rapidly, with a very tight-lipped and army-like attitude.

As she got nearer, Sandra noticed the woman's hard eyes, glittering behind her spectacles, and the thought that flew through her mind was a line from a song ...*you've seen that kind of eyes look at you from underneath a rock*...Toby, on his part, had a flash of recognition, as he remembered the last customer in Bridget's shop the day before. Then they were face to face with her, and the harpy—because that was what she reminded them of—wasted no time in starting in on them,

"So! Here you are. How is it possible that three so vile and despicable youths can look so innocent and blameless? But then again, that is the marks of the devil's apostles: looking innocent while misleading and depraving others! Filthy little demon spawn! And that poor, misguided, nice man.

"What wrong had he done to take up with you three, only to be cast into the abyss like that?"

Somehow detached from the situation at hand, Toby and Roger noticed people standing silently along the sides of the street, some looking at their accuser with approval, some with distaste, but all being quiet, like they could not disturb while a higher authority was speaking. Sandra, on the other hand, was fuming and getting ready to throw her own explosion into their accuser's face. Toby, noticing this, quietly laid a hand on her shoulder while whispering into her ear, "Let it go, she is not worthy of a reply." The three of them continued walking, not answering her at all, but that did not deter her from keeping up the scolding—or public persecution—she had started.

"I know what you have done, you murderous little vermin! That poor, gullible, but lovely man, going to his death because of your despicable actions!" She was catching her breath, ready to start another outpouring of hateful bile, when the village shop front door opened, and Bridget Waters made her appearance on the top step.

"At it again, are you, Mrs Reignan?" Her voice was soft, but cold, and the icy stare that met the harpy's glowing eyes eventually made them flicker and look away. Mrs Reignan then backed off a few steps and like the lifting of a poisonous fog, her spell on the crowd was loosened. It started to disperse as the three friends made their escape into the welcoming warmth of the shop, leaving Mrs Reignan staring spitefully after them.

Just as the three friends disappeared into the shop, a car bearing the logo of the local newspaper pulled up outside the library, and a journalist and a photographer jumped out of it and went in search of the librarian, whose name they had been given by the police. Sissel was ready to lock up when they arrived, but sighting deeply inwardly, she let them in and sat down to answer their questions as well as she could or dared. She had a sinking feeling that this was only the first trickle of what would become a tsunami. If Toby and his friends had known this, they might have been seen running into the forest again, but for now they were blissfully unaware. She made up her mind to call Sandra as soon as she had the chance of doing so unobtrusively.

Once they were on the inside of the door, the mood they had been under was almost magically lifted too, and they set down their backpacks as Bridget locked the door behind them. Then she guided them into the back room where there were mugs of cocoa with whipped cream on top, wonderful, hot cheese sandwiches, and little tumblers with what looked suspiciously like whisky in them, all laid out for them on the round table in the centre of the room. Smiling, she bid them sit down and throw off their worries while they ate, and they had no problems doing just that. Wolfing his way into the third sandwich, Roger realised how hungry he had been, their lunch in the glen on the mountainside was but a distant memory, and that was actually many hours ago, he realised. He looked up, a little guilty at the way he was eating, but that feeling was soon eased: the other two were going at it the same way, and Bridget was sitting there, smiling at the way they did justice to her spread. When the hunger abated, and they had satisfied their inner wolves for now, they all settled back in their chairs, nipping at the whisky, and drinking their cocoa with relish. Bridget looked at each of them, nodded and simply said: "Tell me."

At first, they were hesitant, stumbling over words, breaking off in the middle of sentences, and constantly interrupting each other. This only lasted for a few minutes, though, and they soon got their story going, telling their parts of it in as nearly a linear fashion as possible. Bridget was listening to them, for the most part with her eyes closed, and with lines of worry etching their way into her face as they progressed with their tale. At the end, when everyone seemed to have exhausted the topic, Toby showed Bridget the rune carvings he and Roger had found and asked her if she could decipher them. To his shock, he found Bridget's eyes filling with tears, and when she put her hands on the table, there was a slight tremor to them. She just sat there quietly without speaking, looking into...somewhere else altogether? Toby was getting nervous again and was just getting ready to ask her if she was alright, when she turned her eyes on them again, and her face turned grim and determined. She stood up, told them all to remain seated, and disappeared into the adjoining room, where they could hear her opening and shutting drawers and getting something out of a closet before returning to them.

Meanwhile, they were just sitting there bewildered and not just a little alarmed, anxious about what was to come, but then she returned carrying a huge, voluminous book and other paraphernalia in her hands. Slamming the book down on the table and putting the other stuff down next to it, she then sat down, put her spectacles on her nose and stared at them for a few seconds over the rim of the glasses before turning to the book. In the light of the candles on the table, Toby realised, she was looking more than just a little like the image of the village witch that he had in his head. *This is for real!* he thought, and then Bridget cleared her throat. When she opened the book, slowly, almost reverently, they all held their breath, as if they were somehow afraid to desecrate the moment. Then she started reading, and for a moment both Toby and Roger felt cheated and disappointed: she sounded so normal! It was as if she was reading a bedside story for a child, nothing more, nothing less.

But then they started to pay attention to what she was telling them, and what they heard caused their hair to stand straight out from their scalps, at least that is what it felt like. What she said was quite simply terrifying, there was no other word for it, and with everything they had experienced that day—and the previous days—they knew it was real, as real as the chairs they were sitting on. Sandra, who was more experienced in this part of reality than either of them, was sitting still, looking like a little girl, with bowed head and crying softly. Without thinking, Toby put his arm around her shoulders to comfort her, and she let it stay as they listened to Bridget's voice, telling them the secret she had been harbouring and how it affected their own predicament as well.

"The being known as Draugen, that pulls people and boats under, are in essence the same creature as Noekken that does the same in waters and lakes, and Fossegrimen that haunts the waterfalls. All of them are creatures of fairytales and sagas and are thought to be creatures of myth and imagination, which had come into being for the purpose of explaining disappearances and deaths that were inexplicable. But behind them all lie the god of old, the Vane; Njord, and his fellow god Aegir. Aegir is the name of the god of the sea, but Njord was the one who brought good fortune to those who sailed it. You could say they were collaborating in a way. With his power over the water in all its forms, Aegir helped shape and rule the landscape through the power of water and ice. Njord's favourite abode was in his stronghold by the sea, Noatun, but when the humans unknowingly invaded his lands, he retreated into the halls beneath the ice, where no enemy could enter, and there he stayed on, cloaking himself in sheets of snow and the ages-old ice of the glaciers." She looked up from the book, lights twinkling in her spectacles and bouncing back in their eyes. Then she removed her spectacles and put them down before looking at them again, this time with compassion and sorrow in her eyes: "That is who you are looking for, who you are trying to force into the open, who you are trying to battle. I suspected it when you told me of your experiences, but what brought it home to me, was the rune inscription that you photographed, Toby. It is a warning, left behind thousands of years ago. A warning to everyone who came here, to turn around and go back where they came from, for this was Njord's land, and he wanted to rest and be left alone! You do know where the name 'Nordheim' comes from?" Three blank stares met her eyes. "It comes from old Norse. Njord's home in old Norse is "Njords heima", and in modern Norwegian that has become Nordheim!"

That statement left them speechless. Toby could feel his heart trying to hammer its way out of his chest, while his mind was protesting madly, insisting that they were half mad to believe her. *And what about my own eyes?* he thought to himself. His mind had no reply, and its protests seemed rather feeble after that. Roger had similar difficulties, trying to fit these statements into his normally quite rationally minded intellect, proved to be hard, but then again, what were the options? Sandra dried her tears and met Bridget's gaze over the table, smiling weakly. Bridget looked them all in the eyes before continuing: "I am very much afraid for you now, for you have provoked the power of old and there is no saying if he will let you live—much less let you leave—with the knowledge of his existence." The silence that fell was like a thundering waterfall, drowning out every attempt at rational thought, filling them with a fear so deep, it took their breath away completely. They just sat there open-mouthed, staring at her with wide, bulging eyes, forgetting to breathe, drying, no, shrivelling up, like flowers wilted in the frost of spring. Toby's heart was racing at breakneck speed, he tried in vain to moisten his lips by licking them, but his mouth was as dry as the outside of his skin. He poured a glass of water for himself, steadying his hand with the other to avoid spilling it, he was shaking so badly. Then, after he had drunk it, he was finally ready to ask the question they were all struggling with in their mind: "I'm...We're..." he took a deep breath and started over: "is there anything—anything at all—we can do to placate the force we have awakened? We never meant to start a war, we were just looking for answers...and wound up getting far more than we bargained for...I am sorry!" He looked down at his hands, and then at the floor, tears stinging in his eyes and his throat constricting as if he was being strangled.

Sandra placed a hand over his in a gesture of sympathy and care and looked at Bridget. Her eyes were silently pleading for help, and slowly Bridget nodded in reply.

The very first thing she did, was replenishing the water and the whisky tumblers. Then, when she sat down again, she was fingering a necklace that had hitherto lain hidden under her sweater. When it was brought into the light, they could all see that it was an amulet of sorts, but it was Roger who recognised it for what it was. It was a beautiful piece of jewellery, looking like a ring on a chain. "Brisingamen!" he said loudly, "Froya's necklace!" Bridget smiled: "Excellent," she said, "you remember the things you learned so long ago in primary school! Froya, the daughter of Njord. She is exactly who you must turn to for protection—Njord's daughter, war goddess, leader of the Valkyrie, and the goddess of fertility, growth and love." She was smiling fully at them now, and at that moment she looked more than human, her eyes shining, stars twinkling in their depths, but then the moment was gone. "Explain what we must do, please!" said Sandra.

Meanwhile, Mrs Reignan was sitting in the living room of Mrs Thorsten, having a cup of tea, and feeling thoroughly pleased with herself. The church club had gathered after the appalling events this day, to discuss how they should handle it, what kind of reactions that would be necessary and proper, and to make plans for the expected upcoming media storm. They needed to be prepared for anything, as the media—useful tools they might be—could easily go off on a different path from what they should be on. The club consisted of most of the wealthy farmers from the area, Mr Starby being the most prominent, some of the old families, of which she herself was a representative, and of course the minister and laymen connected with the church. The minister could not be found when they arranged this hasty meeting. *He is probably occupied with strategies for the coming days,* she thought. In addition to the aforementioned people, there were also the representatives from the two biggest businesses in the village: Mrs Kingsman, from Hotel Daleswood, and Mr Rowan, from the Fjordsuite Hotel.

The discussion was, as one would expect in such a civil society, respectful and low-key. Carefully sipping their tea, they spoke in measured tones and with the utmost care to use the right wording and the correct phrasing to avoid stirring up any undue emotional responses. Right now, they were discussing how this could be used as a good thing for the village. "I think," said Mr Rowan, "that if we handle this the right way, we could see an inflow of tourists, seeking to feel the mystery and beauty of the nature. If we could just tone down the deaths and focus on the mystical essence, it would work out fine."

"Yes," said Mrs Kingsman, "but you would have to keep your tongue when addressing the media: They will jump on any references to a mystical source in connection with the tragic deaths!" Mrs Reignan nodded in agreement. "I agree," Mr Starby said. "If we could find someone in this congregation who could be a spokesman for us all, then we could work on some statements that we may use in the media."

This last led to some vigorous stirring of tea, and the sipping of teacups got quite audible while everyone thought frantically, or perhaps cynically, over who that person might be. It should be someone with a high moral standing and good oratory gifts, who at the same time were charismatic and trustworthy in appearance. Someone who could show sympathy and empathy, yet at the same time be crystal clear about how things were, or not were, connected. The discussion lasted till late afternoon, but in the end, they had decided that Mr Starby would be the spokesperson, and they had also settled some of the statements that he would give to the media when called upon. *All in all, a good day's work. The very last thing they did before breaking up, was to say a prayer for Kenneth Barker's soul. A very decent thing to do,* Mrs Reignan thought, and *highly needed, she could add.*

All of these events were completely lost on Sofie, who was slowly coming to, lying on the ground in a clearing inside the woods. When she awoke, she was confused and bewildered, but then she started to remember what had happened just before 'the lights went out' as her cousin, Roger Brigstad, would have phrased it, and she nearly lay down again. Reality held her back though, and she slowly rose to her feet. She knew she had to get back to 'civilization' before the dark fell and she could get completely lost. Brushing herself down, she picked up the bucket, now completely empty—a*t least the cows got the good stuff,* she thought, and started to retrace her steps down the mountainside. It proved to be more difficult than it should have been, even given the lack of clear view inside the forest. Somehow, the path seemed to have disappeared, and the bushes were unyielding where she wanted to go. Struggling and out of breath, she made a halt and wondered what was happening to her: she was not this out of shape?!?

While she stood there, it got considerably darker under the trees, and she began to get worried, starting to think that a thunderstorm was building up rapidly. There were plenty of signs apart from the sudden darkness. The wind was picking up, and the rising electricity in the air was making the hairs on her arms stand straight out, and she could feel the hair on her scalp trying to do the same. She looked around, feeling distinctly nervous, looking for somewhere—anywhere—she could take shelter from what felt like an upcoming whopping round of thunder, lightning, and rain. That was when she became aware of the sounds of cracking twigs. It seemed to come from everywhere at once, and it was growing louder and more insistent by the minute. Now seriously spooked, she cried out in a voice she hardly recognised as her own: "Who's there?" but no answer came.

Panic threatened to take hold, but she fought it back, knowing that to panic up here equalled broken bones from nasty tumbles when you ran wild, yet it was all she could do to keep her feet from dashing away with her. Before long, though, she wished she had let them have their way. Between the trees she could make out the outline of a man. That name did not do him justice though, because he was more of a giant, reaching more than halfway up the length of the trees, and looking wide enough to break the wind. He was standing perfectly still, just looking at her, studying her, with his head slightly tilted to one side. He did not look dangerous, precisely, but something in his stance gave the impression of immense power—not just physical—and self-reliance: he did not give a damn what other people thought or felt about him. Then he took one step forward and his face came into view, bearded and ruggedly good looking, but with the most intense eyes she had ever seen, blue-green and ice cold. She froze up, then turned to dash away, panic now fully in control of her, but it was too late. She felt his hand on her neck, strong and hot, and fainted clean yet again.

Chapter 9

John Peregrine, the minister, had been one of the first people to arrive at the library when the news of the accident became known. He had witnessed the three of them, shocked and almost paralysed, coming slowly towards the librarian who were out meeting them. When they disappeared inside, he followed, unobtrusively of course, and positioned himself so that he could watch and listen in on their conversation as much as possible. The conference rooms were not soundproof, he knew that from earlier visits. Not that he would eavesdrop on purpose. God forbid that he should do such a thing—eavesdropping was a sin—but he could still catch quite a bit of the following conversation. During the time he lingered there, he learned about some of the particulars surrounding the accident, and he knew at once that this was the case for which he had been praying: a chance to show them all who was the mightiest: his God or that piece of devilish superstition! The fact that that last part held a contradiction in terms, completely evaded his attention.

He stayed around long enough to watch the mortuary van carry the poor fool away, and then he started on his way back through the village. He was walking slowly, though, and so he was witness to the run-in with Mrs Reignan. Standing on the sidewalk, in the shadow of the local menhir or runestone, he watched as she started her rant, scolding the three young people in front of her, almost flaying them, he thought. He did not find her quite right in her assessment of the three, though. He thought they were misguided, young people who had strayed from the path of the righteous, the path to salvation. But it was not too late to bring them back into the fold! A show of strength, a victory for his Lord, that was what could convince them to turn away from the path of the wicked, of this he was morally sure! Smiling to himself, he quietly faded away into the night, moments before Bridget Waters made her entrance on the scene. If he had stayed long enough to witness that, he would have had more than enough fuel to fan his determination through the night. That woman was a witch, of that he was certain, but she was too well liked in the village to start a fight with. She was probably too well educated too, which would have given him a few more headaches and challenges than he bargained for, so he had wisely decided to let her be, at least for the time being.

He walked into his annex with the step and gait of a man with a purpose. Taking off his hat and cloak and hanging them on their accustomed pegs, he went into his study. He had a lot of studying to do if this venture was going to have the outcome he desired, and so he got out his books, religious items, and writings that he needed for the preparation. Many of these paraphernalia were of such a nature, that if his congregation had known, they would have fled the church immediately. Which was why he kept it a secret, of course. To be able to appreciate these writings and tools, you had to have a deep understanding of demonology, and he had studied the subject for over thirty years, always having been interested in the topic, much to his father's displeasure, even when he was a young lad. His father had been a clerk in the church office in a small town, and he had a much sunnier view of what religion was or should be. John Peregrine scoffed at that, religion was no laughing matter, and even the bright events in the church year were fraught with danger, pain, and remorse. But why was he thinking of these long-gone things now? He was feeling a bit irritated with himself. *Now, John* he thought to himself, *enough of this nonsense. You will never be prepared for the job at hand if you do not get started now!* He shook off the interrupting thoughts and the feeling of unease that always came with them and got down to work.

Mrs Reignan, meanwhile, was in bed already. Beauty sleep before midnight, and early bird gets the worm: those were the adages her mother had lived by, and young Charlotte had heard them over and over until they were stuck in her brain, forever echoing the voice of her mother. But it worked for her, and as she closed her eyes and got ready to dream the dreams of the righteous, she smiled. The change in her expression would have shaken anyone who knew her to the core; she looked happy, genuinely happy. She sighed deeply, a sign that she was entering the dream mode of sleep, and as the dream unfolded and her eyes began their characteristic rapid eye movement that is the tell-tale sign of dreaming, her expressions changed with the flow of images in her brain. Toward the end of the dream cycle, she seemed to be disturbed by something: her face frowned, her eye movements got frantic, and her breathing became laborious and rapid. A nightmare visited her dream, shaking her up and causing distress, but when she managed to shake herself awake at last, she could not remember what it had been about. Going to the kitchen for a glass of water, she blamed her nightmare on the events of the day, and then she went back to bed.

Sleep eluded her for almost an hour, though.

At the same time, Bridget was finishing her instructions in front of three alternately blushing and paling customers. Sandra felt feverish—she was shivering and sweating a little—but if that was a fever symptom, an anticipatory feeling, or perhaps a reaction of fear, she did not know. The thought that kept repeating in her mind, was: "How can she expect us—me—to do that? I mean, I do not even know him, really…" At the same time as she was profoundly shocked—to the core of her being—she was also aware that this might be their only shot at surviving the ordeal before them. In fact, it almost certainly was, but still…She looked at Toby, almost shyly, then turned away blushing. Roger, on the other hand, was just sitting there, shell-shocked, his mind whirling with the information he had just been given. He felt empty, like he had been shaken until all the contents had leaked out, and he was ready to be filled…with what? He could not say, and he was not ready to discuss it with anyone, not even Toby, not yet anyway. Toby, as shocked and shaken as the other two, was just sitting there thankful for the candlelight setting: he was blushing and paling and felt like a fool. His little secret threatened to choke him now, the secret that had grown more and more sore and acidic to his self-esteem over the years, the one he barely could admit to himself. He was a male virgin. He had never, ever confided in anyone, it was too big and threatening, somehow. But now it would have to come out…Oh, why? *It would be easier to just jump in front of a bus!* he thought, but then he smiled ruefully at himself: *Since there are precious few buses that run in Nordheim, you will have to go for option one,* he said to himself, and then his mouth dried out again.

The silence between the three lasted and lasted, thickening by the minute, until the dam burst, and they all started talking at once, loudly and hectically. Then the absurdity of the situation hit them, and they started sniggering, then giggling, then laughing, and in the end, they were hee-hawing like a trio of donkeys, tears rolling down their cheeks. Bridget was just sitting there, smiling enigmatically. She knew where the laughter came from, and she preferred this way of releasing their tension to wailing and crying, as a lot of people would have done in the same situation.

"I'm sorry," said Roger, drying his tears, "but this seems to be our way of handling things in general. It is not the first, nor will it be the last time we crack up during this ordeal!"

"Just what I was going to say," Toby chimed in. Sandra was too busy drying her face to say anything, she was still giggling. Eventually, they came to order, still holding their midriffs and drying their tears. The laughter had set them free, at least for the time being, and now they felt ready to enter the unknown—so to speak. "Bridget, I want to thank you for all the help you have given us." said Toby, "it's been invaluable!"

"Well, I can't say that I've been of much help," countered Bridget, "I could not foresee who you were going up to meet, and as a witch with long experience and more solid knowledge of the area, I should have been up to that task."

"Sush!" Sandra sounded strict: "You could not foresee that, no-one could, and you have been nothing but helpful." Bridget smiled warmly in return, then said, with sadness in her eyes: "Poor Kenneth, he really was a ray of sunlight on any dreary day. I am going to miss him a lot!" Nodding in agreement, they rose from their chairs and got ready to leave. "You may leave your gear in the store, just put it in the back room," said Bridget smilingly. "I don't think you need to bring it with you now!"

"No, definitely not!" said Roger, quite a bit friskier now that he had started: *It's that dratted mile before the threshold!* he thought to himself as he followed Toby and Sandra through the store and out in the warm, fragrant night.

Once outside the shop, they stood there for a moment just looking at each other. "She said we should go to the pub and find us a nice, secluded space to ourselves," Sandra said, breaching the silence that had grown between them. "Yes, let's go before I lose my nerve!" Roger answered. Toby could nearly hear his own body screaming for help, but then he managed somehow to put it into motion when the other two started walking. Together they set out for the pub, to fill their minds with something else than the current situation. Bridget had recommended this, because handling the thoughts and emotions after the day's events, would be easier in a crowded environment than in a room by themselves. "And it might also facilitate the assignment I have given you," she added as they walked out the door, making Toby smile weakly when he left.

When they arrived at the pub it was more than half full, but they had no problem finding seats this time either. Entering the room, they could feel the weight of multiple stares on their back, but there were no comments or sounds of obvious displeasure. The pub went noticeably quiet, though, and they felt a bit awkward walking in. In the back of the room, there was a booth with room for six people, and they quickly laid claim to it. That is, Roger laid claim to it, while Toby and Sandra approached the counter to order drinks. Much to their relief, the bartender did not bat an eye when they placed their order, and the rest of the crowd—though some of them had been present at the library—turned out to be decent enough to leave them in peace, as the conversations started up again, at least for the moment anyway.

Decency was perhaps the motivation behind the villagers' treatment, but it had nothing to do with the absence of the reporters, that was down to the librarian, Sissel Davik, and her keeping them, delaying them, until it was too late for them to go searching for the three. But of course, they would be back, together with many others from newspapers, TV-stations, and such, and that was the reason she called Sandra on the phone just as the trio sat down by the table. It was a short conversation, but they got the essentials and all three of them thanked her for the job she had done, keeping the wolves from their doorstep and giving them a much-needed break to make their getaway.

Settling down with their beers, they could feel the terror and anxiousness slowly begin to evaporate through their skin as they sipped and talked. There was so much to discuss, so much to handle, but this was 'left for another day' as Roger put it.

Instead, what they talked about was their plans, places they had been or wanted to visit, friends they had not seen for a long, long time, childhood memories, and Kenneth. Sandra had a few memories of him—only a few—but she also had stories, stories that Olaf had told her over a cup of tea or coffee when she came to visit. Many of these were hysterically funny, while others showed Kenneth's serious side. He had truly been a deep thinker and had some strong views on why he was doing the job he did, what he wanted to accomplish, and what he wanted the world to see and understand. After one of these stories, they all had a quiet moment and toasted Kenneth's memory, then, as Sandra got ready to start on another one, they heard a young woman call out Roger's name.

That woman turned out to be a teacher at the local village school, Janet Johnston by name, who was an acquaintance of Roger's. She had just turned 30 in the beginning of summer, and Roger had some lively stories from that party. As they all were by now a little inebriated, those stories got livelier by the minute, and the laughter rang free and easy, despite the circumstances. Or perhaps because of them: the need to take a step back from a difficult situation and get some distance between yourself and it, is a very human reaction. Some of Janet's other acquaintances also joined their party, when they saw first-hand, that the trio was neither dangerous nor treacherous. The party turned louder and louder, as the laughter that emanated from the group was contagious and infected the whole pub. There were people who had problems with this kind of behaviour, of course, but those that took an issue with this, left the pub early. They did cast some dark and disapproving glances toward the group, but these went largely unnoticed.

As the evening progressed, however, it became clear that as far as Janet was concerned, the storytelling and the singing that was now also being introduced, was of no interest whatsoever. She was deeply concerned over the effect the day's incidents could have had on Roger and was using every opportunity she could to interrogate him and assure him that she was there for him if he needed to confide in someone. It could have been embarrassing, but because she was so earnest, it all seemed natural, like it was meant to be. She clearly had a soft spot for Roger, maybe more than one, and as the evening progressed into night, he could feel his soul—so empty a few hours ago—being filled with something new, something unfamiliar, but good. He did not find it unpleasant, Janet fussing over his well-being, it felt so good and warm, and like…home? By now she was sitting on his lap—all the seats were taken—kissing him softly on the lips. Sandra and Toby, who had at some time during the evening begun holding hands, looked at each other and nodded without a word.

Quietly and as unobtrusively as they could, they left the party behind and slipped out into the warm night air. They had observed what had begun to happen, and now they smiled secretly to each other as they strolled along the street.

They strolled slowly through the fragrant night, passing from the village itself and onto the country lane, not really having a goal or a place they had to be. The only thing they were conscious of, was the night around them: deep, soft, dark, but brilliant at the same time. And silent, every sound muffled, yet at the same time clearly audible. To top it off, the only sounds in the night were those of the night itself, where you could hear the scuttling back and forth of animals rustling in the forest next to the road.

Walking along, holding hands, and just smelling the fragrance of growing, living plants, and listening to the sounds of life, they found that their feet had left the road behind, and they were now strolling through the meadows and entering the canopy of the forest. As they had no goal, no place they needed to be, they allowed themselves to be swallowed by the soft darkness, the stars lighting their path. There was no fear, no nervousness, no stress involved, it was just natural with an air of enchantment in it.

None of them said a word, and yet they felt like they had spoken volumes, walking silently in a floral field on the outskirts of the forest. It was not the pine forest from earlier, this was a forest of leafy trees—birch, ash, asp, and such—crowned with an abundancy of leaves in all hues of green, from the lightest to the darkest, shielding them from the mountain and the menace that they now knew was there.

Entering the forest in earnest, they were not alone. Something unseen was following them, ever so silently. It made ripples in the grass, like a cat running; a troll cat it would have been called by the elderly folks. It could also be likened to waves in an ocean, spreading around them, playing, and frolicking like playful dolphins, or it could maybe be puppies, playful and clumsy. A kind of magic feeling was permeating the air and everything around them. Both Toby and Sandra could sense it, but unlike earlier, they did not feel threatened by it. This was a kind of benevolent magic, a magic so ancient it seemed to flow through all things, both those which we consider living, like plants, animals, and such, but also the 'dead', like minerals, stones, and other materials. It made them feel elated.

Moving between the trees they came to a glade, a clearing or opening in the forest. It lay there—a pond in the forest green—bathed in the clear and strong moonlight, with the flowers all open, as if it was daylight. On a patch in the middle of the clearing, they sat down. The ground was covered in deep, soft, dry moss, which felt like down when they leant back in it, turning their faces to the moon. The moon was dazzling, blinding them with its silvery light as they stared straight into it. It was not just a full moon, but it was as close to the earth as it could be, and therefore bigger than any of them had seen it before. In addition, it was a red moon. Not the red of danger or war, but the red of love—a lover's moon. Lying down in that soft moss and enjoying the peaceful stillness of the night, they felt all their worries finally leaving their bodies. It was a wholesome feeling, relaxing on the ground, surrounded by nature and nature's creatures, just feeling blissful after what they had experienced earlier. Their arms touched, just a little, but Toby felt like he had been electrified. In fact, he felt like the whole world had been electrified and was buzzing with energy about to explode. He realised that he was holding his breath, lying completely still, lest he break the spell that was over him. Then he felt Sandra sitting half up and saw her shadow leaning over him. Or—was it Sandra? Her eyes were shining with the moon reflected in them, and he felt his mind swim in those eyes while a stubborn part of the rational, old Toby insisted that her eyes could not reflect the moonlight: the moon was behind her! Her voice came to him, warm, whispering: "Here, there is nothing that can hurt you. With my blessing you can go everywhere, on land, on sea, and in the air. As long as you stay true!"

The feeling inside him was partially awe, partially bliss, and partially pure joy as he nodded and said "Yes." When she kissed him, he could have sworn he heard a chorus of glad voices singing, but then he kissed her back, and in that precious night, a new life began for them both.

The contrast between that sacred feeling in the field and the interior of the annex could hardly have been greater. In his study, John Peregrine was busy making the last preparations for his mission, one that would bring about the end of these horrible events, and at the same time restore the church's foundation in the village, bringing the flock back into the fold—so to speak. He had felt the anger rising inside him as he was contemplating the events that were going on—in his village—and he was literally gritting his teeth as he packed the last items into his backpack. But now he would not allow this to go on any longer, he was going to take charge of the situation and drive the demons that were behind it, right back to hell, where they belonged! He had God, the Almighty, on his side: how could he possibly lose!? The very last item to be put in his pack, right on top of the Bible, was a small flask of Holy Water from Rome. It had been blessed by His Holiness, the Pope himself, and John felt convinced that nothing could stand against the power of this, no matter how powerful the demon may be! Checking for the last time, he felt sure that everything that he might be needing on this crusade, was included in his pack.

He then put on his sturdy mountain shoes, went out of his house, locking the front door behind him, and set his course for the treacherous cliff, feeling greatly elated and excited: He was heading for glory, he just knew it, and it was going to be so sweet! In the warm, fragrant night, he could almost hear a choir of angels singing, sending him off to do the Lord's bidding and be victorious! As he started on his hike up the mountain side, he was unfortunately too preoccupied to hear the choir as it sounded more and more anxious and was replaced by another choir that Toby, Sandra, and Roger knew all too well. A few minutes after he reached the line of trees and disappeared into them, you could still hear the ominous sound of the male voices, sinking slowly into the range below human hearing.

Chapter 10

During his climb up the steep mountainside, John Peregrine had ample time to think about the situation and preparing himself for it. But his thoughts refused to obey him, and he found himself thinking about his past and how one thing had led to another, all pointing towards this moment as the apotheosis. All his endeavours, all his overcome obstacles, they had prepared him for this moment, made him stronger, more aware, and more equipped for whatever lay ahead. His student years at the seminary, with the constant bickering between the teachers and the idealistic students, the first years of service, when he felt his burning faith and energetic preaching being drowned in a pool of complacency, and his father's disapproval of his chosen path, all that had merely strengthened his resolve. Now he was in the place where he was meant to be, with a small but intensely loyal congregation, getting ready for the biggest, most significant sermon of his life, the exorcism of the evil that lay behind the occurrences in this village!

After finishing his climb, catching his breath, and wiping his sweat, John Peregrine took a moment just admiring the view from up there in the mountainside. The whole village and its surroundings were laid out beneath his feet, shining like a gem in the bright moonlight, filling his heart with joy. Mixed in with that joy was pride, and not just a little, but that was something he would never admit, not even to himself. He was proud of his work in the village, and of his efforts to bring in the rest of the flock that was running wild. Although the results so far had been slim, almost non-existent to tell the truth, yet he felt convinced that it was only a matter of time. He had sown his seed, and some of it would have fallen on fertile ground, even if some of the recipients made their hearts hard and their fields barren. Now, that was the beginning of a sermon! Now, standing there, lost in his thoughts, and relishing the clear night with a full moon and when that set: a million shining stars, he would not have noticed a herd of elephants walking by, so perhaps he was excused for not noticing the rustling in the bushes. It ceased as quickly as it had started, so when he snapped out of his reverie, any trace of anything untoward was long gone.

As he set about putting his icons, relics, and religious props into their designated places, he went through the ritual ahead of him for the umpteenth time, practicing parts of it in his head. There was no room for mistakes, even though he saw his god as the superior and himself as an able exorcist. The exorcism that he was going to perform, would bring peace to the village and an end to the endless disappearances and accidents, and this would be done by either binding the demon behind it all to the mountain in which he hid, or by banishing him to hell from whence he came! That was what he hoped at least. That it might lead to hero status for himself was not something he would even dream of vocalising, but somewhere in the back of his head, that thought had found a secure dwelling. What could the future bring for someone who had brought peace to an entire village through his extraordinary skills and perseverance?

Once again, he was lost in his reveries, setting up his last items for the ritual while seeing in his mind how it would play out. If he only would have taken the time to interview the survivors of the last events, he would have known where he was standing and what peril he was in, but as it were, he was blissfully unaware that he was in the exact same spot where Toby and Roger had had their horrifying experience. Had he but used his eyes, he would have recognised the door in the mountain wall and seen the marks on the outside, but he was looking inward, and so the opportunity for a quick exit was lost. Perhaps it was too late, anyway.

At last, everything was ready and set, the only thing missing was his formal attire—the chasuble—which was quickly donned, and then he was ready. As he started the first incantation, he became aware of some slight changes in his surroundings. A sound, that would be all too familiar to the three survivors, had begun to play, like an almost inaudible orchestra. Continuing with the ritualistic prayer, he still felt confident.

Perhaps even more now that he was registering something of the opposition. In his mind he was already savouring the taste of victory, taking the eerie music in the air for one of fear and eventual surrender. Nothing could be further from the truth, but when the sound died away as quickly as it started, his belief in himself and the ritual was strengthened, and he carried on with renewed fervour. Reaching the first ringing climax in the exorcism he took a short breather to let it properly take hold before the next phase began.

In that pause, a new sensation introduced itself and started to build momentum, more sinister than the music that he first had heard, movements in the trees and bushes. It looked as if there was something big walking through them, pushing them out of the way, but nothing could be seen: no bodies, no shadows, nothing at all.

These entities came from all directions—except the mountain wall of course—and they blocked off any escape routes he could have thought of if escape had been on his mind. No, he could not see them, but he could feel them, standing around him like...a prison guard? He felt eyes watching his every move, monitoring his breath even. Still confident—whatever you could say about the minister, and there were plenty who would be more than eager to do just that—his faith and his trust in it, were unflinching. He carried on with his exorcism, sending his voice toward the sky with all the power and youthful enthusiasm he could muster, building up to another crescendo in the ritual. In this exalted state, beads of sweat were running down from his brow and into his eyes, blurring his vision, but he did not care, he was so sure of victory and of his lord that he did not need his eyes to see the entities crumbling before him! He was so close to the climax of the second part of the exorcism now, he just needed to take a deep breath before the last ground-shaking fermata, and then the final part. And in that pause, that short second, a voice intruded upon his daydreams and sent them crashing to the ground. This was a male voice, deep as the oceans and colder than the glacier on the mountains in the north, thundering out of the ground. It sounded like nothing he had ever heard before, nor ever wanted to hear. The voice of a power, an ancient, mighty power, one he could never conceive of, and it left John Peregrine cold, frozen in his very bones. He felt something he had only heard others talk about, something totally alien to his being: he was mortally afraid, not only for, but in his soul.

John Peregrine had often imagined his glorious moments as gems of memory, to be seen and treasured by him only, and that even his most arduous tasks would become diamonds when hardened by time. This one should have been the pinnacle of them all, the apotheosis of his life, but now that the moment was here, he was completely powerless to do anything but stand there and watch and listen. Yes, he tried to protest, to carry on his ritual, to show the power of his lord and saviour, but all he could bring forth was a sort of hoarse croak that only inspired a cold mirth—a faint snicker, more felt than heard. When that voice addressed him, it was filled with contempt to such a degree that he felt totally crushed, ground to infinitesimal bits. In a second, it stripped him of all the dignity he had left, leaving him raw and exposed, thoroughly naked, both as a man and as a man of the cloth. He wanted to cover his ears, to shut it out, but to no avail. It was as if he was hearing it with his ears and in his mind at the same time. It became abundantly clear to him that the owner of this voice did not heed the language or wording of what he considered an upstart, a much younger deity as it were. Nor did he have any regards for this fledgling god's representative. The voice of that ancient being—yet unnamed—was also making crystal clear its anger at being disturbed in such a rude way. He required peace and solitude, but both had been denied him lately, and he was getting impatient as well as furious. Of course, it was not only John Peregrine and his god—they were merely the spark that caused the anger to explode. It was all the people, the humans, who flooded the forests, crowded the mountains, played raucously round on the glaciers, and intruded upon his solitude in every conceivable and unconceivable way. This last antic was just the last straw.

While John Peregrine stood there, frozen to the spot, drowning in the wrath and bitterness that voice carried, he suddenly became aware that he heard water? It was coming from somewhere close, a bubbling, merry sound, like there was a brook or perhaps a spring nearby. In his terrified state, the only thing he wanted, was to get out of there, but he was unable to move. He just stood there, frozen to the spot, when he became aware that he could no longer feel his feet. Had they been frozen to ice?

Struggling to bend his head, he managed to peek down towards his toes. First, he noticed that there was water covering his feet, or at least the bottom of his mountain shoes, and he was bewildered: Where was it coming from? It seemed to come from the ground itself, but that was impossible, the ground underneath him was solid rock! He tried to lift his feet, to get out of the unpleasant wetness, which was when he realised something horrible: He could not see them! He was…sinking? Slowly, it dawned on him: His feet had somehow sunk into the solid rock as if he were standing on quicksand, and as he watched, his eyes bulging in horror, his ankles slid into the stone. Panic, together with intense pain, flooded his mind, his entire being screamed in agony, and he wanted to flail his hands and holler for help, but not a sound managed to escape, and his limbs remained frozen. Dumb he might be, but his screams of agony could still be heard in the minds of those present. Unfortunately for John Peregrine, none of them were feeling merciful, thus the only thing he could do, was observe his own silent, slow merging with the rock beneath him as he sank into the mountain itself. His terror and pain did not go unnoticed by the might behind the voice either, so his last moments, filled with excruciating torture, were accompanied by laughter, a roaring, brutal hard mirth, that followed him into the darkness, the last thing he heard as merciful oblivion descended upon him.

In the field down in the village forest, two people lay quietly, just relaxing and relishing the closeness of another body next to themselves. The field was still starlit, with the Milky Way spreading out above their heads, but in the east could be seen the faint glimmer of the early late-summer sunrise, still a few hours away. Toby hardly dared to open his eyes, he was afraid that this moment was just a dream and that everything that he had felt for the last hours was just wishful thinking. But he had to look, had to see if Sandra was still there. When he turned over on his side however, and looked down on her face, he found her crying. Totally shocked, all he could do was ask: "What have I done?!? Oh, Sandra, please don't…I will get it right, I…" She stopped his mouth with a soft and joyful kiss: "Toby, all tears are not ill: Some are tears of happiness, and that's what these are. I am crying for joy, for having found you!" Dumbstruck, all he could do was stare at her, but then a smile lit up his face from deep within, and he returned the kiss with an intensity that said it all. "It feels kind of like a storm, a really gruelling, wild, hard storm has passed over me—us—and now we look at a new dawn…That sounds pathetic out loud, it sounded much better inside my head!" Toby groaned, half ashamed of spoiling the moment's magic feeling, but then Sandra laughed. It was that deep, hearty laugh, that nonetheless had the sound of bells in it, and as always, it made him smile, and then chuckle himself. "I think it sounded beautiful," she said, "and it was just the right description!"

Their limbs entwining again, they enjoyed a bit more of each other's kisses, while the fragrant night around them embraced them in a warm cocoon and the sounds of nocturnal animals and insects on the prowl for food, serenaded them into the slowly approaching sunrise. In the end though, they had to get up and move. With sunrise quickly blossoming in the east there would soon be people on the road, and if they were seen coming out of the wood? Well, they did not really like to think of the talk that could bring about! When they exited the forest, so tightly wrapped around each other they looked like some sort of fused, symbiotic creature, they could see Janet and Roger emerging from a glen on the other side of the road. The two couples halted for a moment, silently recognising each other, and then they smiled and went on their way, treading the path that led them to a bed and much needed rest at the end.

Toby and Sandra talked as they strolled along, about the events of yesterday and the wonderful, magical experience of the night. When they found out that, they had both had the same vision while laying down in the field, they stopped in their tracks and looked questioningly into each other's eyes. "How is that…" Sandra asked, then stopped herself, and placing a finger on Toby's lips, continued: "Let us leave it. Some things are not meant to be known, and I believe this is one of those things. It was an enchanted part of a magical night, and it is something we will never understand, I think." Toby nodded slowly, then he kissed her and made her know that he agreed completely. At the end of the dead-end road that they were currently following, lay the house with Sandra's rented flat, and without any further words they went inside, shut the door, and never looked back. On the other side of the village, Roger and Janet had reached the front door of her house, and when she opened the door, he lifted her up and carried her inside before shutting the door behind him.

As the sun rose, the last stragglers from last night's revelries were braving their way home, with sore heads and unsteady feet, while the farmer's made their way to the cowsheds and barns to start the day. It was a scorcher of a morning: bright, rapidly warming, and with an ever so slight breeze to cool the faces of the early morning joggers that were out and about. The two new couples knew nothing about any of this, they were blissfully slumbering, enjoying sleep like innocent children.

At the time when the four lovebirds fell into Morphei arms, Mr Starby rose from his broken slumber, totally worn out and un-rested. He had had a very strenuous night, dreaming about his task going wrong in at least fifty different ways and waking up in a cold sweat. "The devil is having a field day!" he grumbled as he went to the kitchen to make himself a cup, or perhaps a whole thermos, of coffee. What he thought of as devil's work, others might have called performance anxiety, but he would just huff at such 'new-fashioned ideas'. He sat down at the kitchen table, trying to enjoy, like he did most mornings, the stillness and peacefulness before the rest of the family woke up. This day, that seemed impossible to do, though. His whole body felt as if it was filled with ants, running up and down his arms and legs, and making his stomach queasy. He closed his eyes in exasperation, and just wished the day would pass quickly.

Sissel, the forty-something librarian, had also had trouble sleeping, so she had gotten up at four in the morning and relocated herself to the back porch. She brought a book and a blanket with her and got settled in. As she felt the cool night breeze caressing her temples and drying the sweat off her skin, she could also feel herself gradually relaxing. There she sat, in an old and comfy chair, with her book over her chest, now fast asleep in the cool morning air. Her last thoughts before sleep finally found her, had been about Sandra and her friends. *God, I hope they will be alright! What a dreadful situation they are in. The worst,* she thought, now getting a bit incoherent as sleep was imminent, *is that the worst part of this whole business, I think anyway, has yet to come…*

There were more people who had trouble with sleeping that night. Mr Rowan had been up and working all night, talking to business partners in Asia, and preparing the conversations he would have with his American colleagues later. He did not feel tired at all, there was so much to do and so many 'fires' to be put out if his hotel was not going to take a nosedive as a result of this horrible event! Mrs Kingsman was also in her office, trying to save her hotel from possible disaster in the wake of events, but at the same time she was also a trustee of the book town and the glacier museum, and they were definitely in need of some emergency plans there, so…this day was never going to be long enough for the work that needed to be done. But she would just have to plod on!

Mrs Reignan, on the other hand, had no trouble sleeping. She was snoring away, dreaming big dreams of glory, and enjoying the rest of the self-righteous.

For the second time, Sofie felt herself slowly awakening from her unconscious state. Last time had been up in the mountainside after the shock of that dreadful scream, just the thought of it was enough to bring tears to her eyes. This was different, though. She seemed to have a foggy head when it came to remembering what had happened next: wasn't there a thunderstorm? And a man? She was almost certain, but the fog was everywhere, clouding her memory and making it difficult to think.

She sat up carefully and then banged her head in the ceiling of her car. More confusion as she looked around, but it confirmed what her—now sore—head told her. She was lying in the back of her own car, on top of a pile of blankets. She had no idea where they came from, nor had she any recollection of going down the mountainside to her car, but…she must have, or what? Moving with care, she did not want another bump in the head, she managed to open the door from the inside and crept out. Looking at the terrain, she was surprised to find it dry and unmoved, as if the thunderstorm and wind had never existed. Had it been a dream? She shook her head in bewilderment, got in on the driver's side, started up the car and drove slowly onto the road. As the car turned the first curve, she lost sight of the place where she had been parked, and so she did not see the shadow under the trees, nor the pair of glacier-coloured eyes, staring thoughtfully after her.

Chapter 11

Later that morning, the congregation gathered for their morning prayers in the church, a tradition that Mr Peregrine had started up, and which they were all rather fond of. But when they met up in front of the church, they found—much to their surprise—that the door was locked, and the minister was nowhere to be seen. This initially caused some consternation, but then they thought better of it: he was probably exhausted after praying for the dead man's soul last night, not to mention the three misguided souls that had accompanied him. As his close fellow crusaders, each one of them knew how zealous he was in his pursuit of lost souls. So they decided to call his mobile, but that proved to be out of service. Probably so tired that he had shut it off, they agreed. Their next move was to go over to the annex across the road and knock first on the door, then the windows, but to no avail, there was no response. Mr Starby suddenly said: "Let's check his car!" but in the end, that was also a disappointment. The car was in the garage, alright, but there was no one in it.

By now, they were all starting to feel uneasy. This was not like Mr Peregrine at all, he was always reliable, could always be counted on, and this kind of disappearance without a word…that was not John Peregrine! Eventually, the nervousness that had been brewing, took over, and when someone suggested he could have had a seizure or a fit of some kind, they decided to break open the front door. This door, being solid and sturdy, gave them a few sore shoulders and pains, but in the end, they managed to get it open, only to find nothing at all. Now they were truly worried, all of them, and the discussion about where he might be and what might have happened to him, was beginning to take on some hysterical undertones. Mrs Reignan, who could be counted on to assume the worst in any given situation, suggested that he had gone up in the mountainside "like a true crusader" to "banish the evil that resides up there to the darkest corners of hell!" as she put it. Now, Mrs Reignan was often secretly considered to be a nuisance by many even in the church club, but her words still left many of them dry-mouthed and with an unpleasant feeling in their stomachs. What if she was right this time? Her statement left them standing there, uncertain of what to do, but then Mr Starby spoke up: "We will have to organise a search party at once! If that is where he has gone, then we are certain to find him, either on the way up or the way down. Who among you are able to go with me up to the cliff and above?"

In the end it was decided that a group of twelve men, the youngest and most fit, would be going with Mr Starby, while the women in the group would go across the road to Mrs Kingsman's quarters, where they would wait for news from the search party. They decided unanimously to not call the police or the Red Cross, as they would only "muddy the waters" in Mrs Kingsman's words. When the men set out on their search and rescue mission, the women walked over to the hotel and up to Mrs Kingsman's flat where they settled down. Generous amounts of tea and biscuits were brought to them, as well as sandwiches and cakes, all freshly made, if they felt the need for something to strengthen themselves with.

To keep themselves occupied, the women would eat and drink, talk and discuss a wide range of subjects, and some of them, even do some embroidery, mostly on handkerchiefs. They did not expect any news to come for the first hour, as it would be at least an hour before the party reached the cliff, and then they would need time for searching. To top it off, they would also use an hour getting down again, on the grounds of it being so steep. As the telephone reception was exceptionally bad up there, they did therefore not expect any word from the rescuers until after two hours had passed, and that was the earliest.

Coming back home, Sofie first checked if the condition of the cattle had improved, but no: they were all as dry as a desert, still with those expressions of terror in their eyes. She shuddered and went inside the house, her body feeling strangely heavy, and decided to have a shower before sitting down and trying to figure out what had happened during the night. In the shower, after first spending ten minutes just standing there, relishing the warm water coursing down her body, she opened her eyes to get the shampoo bottle and caught a glimpse of herself in the mirror on the opposite wall. In the mirror, she noticed some scratch marks and small bruises on her thighs and belly, and some even under her breasts. She did not worry much about it, considering the falls she had taken and where she had, evidently, spent her night, but she was still astounded at how many there were, some were even on her ribcage.

Turning around to wash her hair, she presented her back to the mirror, but thankfully she was unable to see what was revealed there. As the shower gradually calmed her down, and the warm water soothed her nerves, she felt more like herself again, but not totally, not yet. Outside, the day was turning out to be another scorcher, with clear, blue sky, not a cloud in sight, and temperatures reaching well over 25°C.

The ladies of the church club, sitting there and talking, trying not to draw any conclusions until they had something tangible to work on, and failing miserably at that, were passing the time as well as could be expected, when one of the ladies, a Mrs Thornson, all of a sudden gave a little shriek: "Look! Who is that?!? He is running like a madman with the devil at his heels! What is going on?!?" All of them, getting to their feet and scurrying to the window to see what she was so excited about, were shocked at what they saw: It was Mr Rowan, and he was indeed running like a madman, that much was evident, tearing through field and arable alike, and with such a horrified look on his face, it made some of the women in the group swoon. Gathering their skirts, and their wits, about them, they ran down the stairs to meet him outside.

They got down into the garden at about the same time Mr Rowan came stumbling over the driveway towards them, looking dishevelled and panicked to the extreme. The shock which was showing on his face: his paper-white skin, stretched across his bones like a mask, the wildly staring eyes, wide as teacups, and with only white and black showing, and the beads of sweat gathering on his forehead, were all tell-tale signs that something gruesome must have befallen him or someone else in the party. When prompted about what had happened, though, he started to cry wildly, and it took a good while to calm him down so that he made any sense to them. Finally, they got the story, although it was in jagged bits and pieces at the beginning.

The men found tracks of John Peregrine immediately after they reached the shelf above the cliff. It was clear that he had been there, his chasuble was lying over a stone, with the bottle of holy water right next to it, cap off and the contents gone. But of the man himself there was no trace to be seen. The men had spread out in the shape of a fan, meaning to proceed with a search through the forest, and Mr Starby would be coordinating them, as he had brought walkie talkies from his van. As an avid hunter, he always had them with him, just in case. He was standing there right next to the chasuble and bottle, giving the last directions to the men, when one of them suddenly screamed in terror. Bewildered, Mr Starby looked up to see if anything was falling on him, only to see the man pointing wildly to where his left foot was resting on the rock. He looked down, met the eyes of John Peregrine, and fainted clean away.

Mr Rowan, who was a part of the search team that was preparing to go into the forest, sprinted to Mr Starby's aid, as did several other of the younger men in the party. Quickly laying Mr Starby comfortably next to a tree, they went back to see what the uproar was about. They noticed that the man who first had made them aware that something was amiss, was being violently ill over by some bushes, and other men were looking after him. When they reached the place where Starby had stood, they looked down, and what they saw, made them all blanch: In the rock was the face of a man in total agony, a man they all knew, sunken into the rock as if it were quicksand. The eyes of John Peregrine were staring upwards to the sky, blindly, as if begging someone to get him out of this hellhole, but it was plain that no one had answered. The uproar following this discovery, which every man, in spite of the feeling of horror, had to see for himself, was total breakdown: men were crying their eyes out, swearing until you could smell the sulphur, praying until their hearts nearly ruptured, but nothing helped. When Mr Starby came to again, and was clear enough to look at what he had been standing on, he gave orders that the fastest runner, which was quickly determined to be Mr Rowan, should run to the ladies and relay the story to them, while the rest of the party would walk down to where the reception was good enough for their mobiles, so that the police could be informed about this horrifying, tragic, and inexplicable incident. The last Mr Rowan saw before he started on his run, was another farmer, from the inner part of the village, standing alone and muttering over and over: "It has all been true, all of it…"

When the police arrived, they did not come alone. On their heels were several media outlets: news stations, newspapers, internet channels, and the like, and the whole village was in uproar. Sandra got a phone call from Sissel, telling her the horrifying news of John Peregrines demise, and the minute that call was ended, Sandra was on the phone to Janet, telling her and Roger that they would have to get out of town, and did they have any good suggestions as to where they could hide.

Toby and she also needed somewhere to stay, so if they had any ideas, all were welcome. As it turned out, Janet had a friend in the nearby town who had a log cabin up in the mountainside on the other side of the fjord. This cabin was without electricity, hot water, and even telephone reception, so they would be very inaccessible there. Janet had been given leave to use this at will, because her friend never did, and if Janet wanted to, all she would be asked to do, was to give a word if something needed repairs. The cabin was indeed old-fashioned, but it was comfortable and large, so they could all stay there together. Janet would go shopping for them all, and then they would meet up at her place and drive together to a secluded parking area, from whence it was half an hour's walk up to the cabin. This being agreed upon, Sandra started packing her stuff, while Toby was picked up by Roger, going up to his house to pack their bags and get back to Sandra as quick as possible. They passed several TV-vans on their way, but none of those signalled them, at least not yet. When the four left the village twenty minutes later, the first knock landed on Roger's front door.

Mrs Reignan was completely stunned. She just sat there, cup half raised to her lips, looking like a freeze-frame in a film. Then, the cup started shaking. It was hardly perceptible at first, but then it became obvious, and in the end, it shook so violently that Mrs Thornson had to remove it from her hand to avoid her hurting herself with the hot tea. Gazing into Mrs Reignan's eyes, she saw something she never would have expected to see. Charlotte Reignan's eyes were filled with silent tears that welled and ran down her face, and in her eyes, she could see a look of despair, disbelief, and a horrible vulnerability. Horrible it was, because it was so completely opposite of anything she connected with this woman, whom she had always seen as staunch, direct, and, if truth be told, more than a little hard and prejudicial. Those two last labels were strictly for herself, though, they would never be told to anyone; she was not socially suicidal!

Waiting up there by the horrific scene, Mr Jonathan Starby had ample time to think. He was suffering from shock and would probably suffer from it for a long time, but he was after all of solid local stock, and so he had begun to order his words and memories so as to be able to give the police a clear and coherent account. Or, as clear and coherent an account as was possible, given the fact that this was a totally inexplicable and confounding event with a tragic outcome. The scene behind him made no sense at all. Bewildered and crying men, walking aimlessly around, or just standing silently in small groups. Two men were standing alone under the canopy on the edge of the clearing. These men were muttering to themselves, but they did not make sense to anyone. *Still, they are probably closest to the truth,* Jonathan Starby thought, *because none of this makes any sense at all.* He let out a sigh and turned his attention to the approaching group of policemen. He noticed that they were followed by a group of journalists and cameramen, sweating their way up the steep hill. *They look like beetles.* he thought, *Dung beetles!* a darker part of his mind whispered, but he refused to listen to it, preparing himself for the ordeal that lay ahead of him. A last, stray thought crossed his mind in the seconds before the police arrived, *when will I have time to mourn?* but he had no answer for that.

In the village centre, Mrs Eleanora Kingsman had made the trip down to the reception area of Hotel Daleswood in a hurry. Of course, it was not far to go, but the speed with which she covered the distance, was amazing. Granted, she was shocked, like all the others, but as she was not as close to Mr Peregrine as the rest of the ladies, she managed to push his fate to the side for the moment and be completely focused on the business of running Hotel Daleswood. On a normal day, she would be smiling and relaxed, having an extremely competent staff, but in this situation, nothing was normal at all. So between handling calls from newspapers and other media, she was ordering rooms prepared for a torrent of journalists while at the same time explaining and soothing distressed guests. Mr Rowan, who had made his exit together with Mrs Kingsman, was now on the other side of the village centre and likewise occupied but having a very young staff who were new to the business, he was close to overheating. In addition, he was suffering from stress and the shock of the discovery in the mountainside, but like Mrs Kingsman, he had to put it aside for the moment. He had no illusions about it staying away, he would have to deal with it sooner rather than later, but for now it would have to take the backseat. There were simply too many people relying on him. When the phone rang for the umpteenth time, he was close to screaming into it, but he held himself carefully in check. Then he heard the voice of Eleanora on the other end and slumped back in his chair while sighing with relief. He had been meaning to phone her up and ask her for assistance, but she had thought of that herself, and was now calling him to offer help in the extreme situation they were facing. He could feel the world gradually settling down into a half-manageable state.

    Mrs Amelia Thornson, who had been taking care of the rest of the ladies still sitting in Mrs Kingsman's living room, finally had a moment to herself. Bringing a cup of coffee with her, she went out on the porch and sat down in one of the chairs that stood there together with a stylish coffee table made out of wrought iron and painted white, with faint stripes of pale pink. Tasteful and subtle, as she would have expected.

Holding her cup in both hands, she looked pensively over at the church. It lay there, quiet, and empty, silent. There was not a sign that the demise of its faithful servant had been registered or reacted upon, it was just an empty shell. She did not formulate any theories about it, that would be for later. But she knew she wanted it to be more than a horrible news story or a piece in a gossip magazine. Perhaps it could be a part of the book she was writing? She would have to think about that, it would be a fantastic turning point or high in her story. The book was her little secret and would probably never see the inside of a book shop or be read in a reading circle, but it was a great outlet for her creative spirit and a way to keep herself occupied. *And perhaps a good way to process what we experienced today,* she thought silently to herself.

Sissel Davik was ready to quit her job on the spot and move to Indonesia to do research in the field of folklore. She had taken so many calls, answered so many questions, and directed untold numbers of requests for information on to the police, that she was not merely exhausted, she was wrecked. She was glad she had made that call to Sandra, because had they been in town, they would have been picked clean by the media before they could even begin to defend themselves. Just as she reached for the water bottle, the phone rang again. Its shrill voice rang through the library's office section, echoing off the walls. Staring at it, she imagined it drowning in a vat of oil, hissing as it went slowly under, but then she thought, *who will know I was even here when they rang? It is not a crime to not answer the phone!* Standing up abruptly, she gathered her belongings, turned off the pc and the lights, and went down to the front entrance where she put up a small poster: "Closed until further notice." Sneaking out the back door, she slithered through the canopy in the backyards on her way home.

The hunt for the survivors from the day before had indeed started, but they seemed to have vanished off the face of the earth, along with the schoolteacher, Janet Johnston. This of course gave fuel to many new conspiracy theories, including Janet being taken hostage by wild and desperate murderers, Janet being the victim of devil worshippers, Janet being the ring master of a hitherto undiscovered witch coven, and so on and on. Another thing, which seemed quite unrelated to the other events, was that the village shop closed its doors. There was a note on the door, saying: "Closed until new proprietor takes over," and Bridget Waters had seemingly left, without so much as a nod to anyone. Toby and company did not have any idea about this, but they could actually watch much of the media circus in the village, from their vantage point on the other side of the fjord. They had to go about ten minutes downhill to get reception on their phones, and this they did every day, just to get a picture of what was going on and how intense it was. Every time they did this, their phones nearly 'popped a plug' to use Roger's words, from text messages, lost calls, mails, and other attempts at contacting them. The only people they chose to inform about their wellbeing, were their parents, and even they did not know where the four were hiding. Toby, having lost both of his parents before he turned 20, felt a little envious at the others, but then he thought of the wonderful girl he had found, and smiled.

Of course, the reporters were not only concerned with the three survivors and fugitives, but they were also on the hunt for other witnesses, Mr Starby being the most wanted. Then there was this gruesome sight up in the mountain, the image of the minister, sunken into the stone. Many were the teams that went up there, looking to get the ultimate shot of the site, but they all came back down again, deeply disappointed. Not because they could not see anything, the face in the stone was still screaming to them in agony, but any pictures that were taken up there ended up being blurry and grey, without any clear image on them. The reason for this was elusive, they could not detect any radiation in the area, but still that was what it reminded them of: radiation that degraded their film. "Of course," one photographer was heard saying, "it should not matter now that most cameras are digital, but something still affects them, rendering any pictures taken up there, entirely useless!"

In the cabin, the days were spent talking together, being silent together, and working through the experience they had shared. Janet, who had not been a part of their dreadful adventure from the start, was now given the full story, and she was astounded as well as terrified. It helped Toby, Roger, and Sandra to retell their story this way, to understand cognitively what they had been through, and to process it properly, so they were glad Janet had the time, the guts, and the presence of mind to listen to them. It turned out that she was a good listener as well as a therapist. Being a teacher, she explained to them, does not only entail teaching, but it also involves psychology, social work, special pedagogics, problem solving, and cognitive therapy, so she was well equipped to be their coach during their stay.

At first, they did not know how long it was going to last before it was relatively safe to creep out of their lair, so they just stayed put. Thanks to Janet, they had enough supplies to dig in for the winter if necessary, so that was not a problem.

However, they hoped to be able to get out and escape the area before cabin fever set in. Three days into their stay, though, they got a visitor. There was a knock on the door, not a loud, but a firm one. All of them froze in their places with a sinking feeling in their bodies: *Oh, no, that was it, we are busted!* was the thought that was running through Roger's mind. Then they heard a voice from the outside: "Open up Toby, I know you are there. This is Axel Hoegh from the police department, and I just want to check on you." Toby felt so relieved he was almost giddy when he opened the door, and welcomed Axel inside. Axel wasted no time: He gave Toby a bear hug of dimensions and proceeded to do the same with the other three, then they sat down around the kitchen table, and Axel started talking.

That is, he started when Janet had provided them all with big mugs of coffee, and put a plate of cookies on the table. Smiling warmly at them all, he first presented the situation in the village as it was right now. "It is bad," he said, "and the media are conducting a veritable manhunt for you, all four of you. They want to hear what you experienced and present a lot of different theories about what it was you saw, and some of them want to make fools of you, of course. It is a wonder they have not issued a bounty on your heads! As for the rest of the village, they are split. Most of them feel sorry for you, and hope that you are all right, some think you have done it on purpose, to get attention, and a few of them see you as devil worshippers and want to bring in the inquisition! When it comes to that second group, the ones who think you have done it for attention, I have asked them if they think you murdered poor Kenneth Barker, and then proceeded to carve poor John Peregrine into the rock.

When I asked them, they went awfully quiet, though." Toby smiled weakly, he had read about the speculations both on Facebook and in the newspapers when he had been down to their reception area.

"But how did you find us?" Janet asked. "It was not easy! I had quite the bit of luck: an old friend of mine, who owns a cabin down by the fjord, mentioned that he knew someone who had a cabin up here, but they were not using it. Still, he had seen smoke from it these last days, and he was starting to wonder. I checked it out with the cabin's owner, and he mentioned that his daughter had an arrangement with Janet about the use of it. So I went back to my acquaintance and told him that it was used by some distant relatives, and then I made the climb up here. And I must say you have got quite the view! If you'd had one of those long-range rifles, you could probably read their lips through the scope on it, right in the middle of the village!"

"Yes, you are right, we could. But as it happens, we have been quite satisfied with the situation as it is: no one has been able to reach us in any way, and we have had peace and time to process what we have been through." It was Sandra who said this, looking a little worried. Toby looked questioningly at her, but then it dawned on him: "Axel is not here to drag us back, he would not do that! Would you?" This last was a question to Axel, who smiled and answered: "No, I would not."

"But why should you care so much about Toby's wellbeing that you came here to check up on him and the rest of us?"

Sandra was not going to let go of the question until she had gotten a thorough answer.

Axel looked down, his eyes staring blankly at the table for a long time, then he lifted his face towards them, and what met their eyes made them jump. Gone were the eyes of the policeman, and his charming smile and good looks, and they were face to face with a being much older, wiser, and more dangerous than anything they had ever encountered in person. The eyes were cobalt blue with a centre as black as coal, lit with a smouldering fire within, and the face was hard, with clearly lined features. He was not bad looking, but he did not seem human anymore. When he spoke again, his voice was deeper, an almost impossibly low bass, that sounded harsher, also he seemed to grow bigger, both taller and wider. "You are safe now," he said, "and you should leave this area for good. Do not try to stay, for I will not guarantee that you will survive a second time." He then turned to Sandra: "You are a good witch, working for what you see as good causes, but a good witch also knows when she should leave well-enough alone. Remember that!" Sandra was shivering all over, white as paper, with wide eyes. She was scared to death. Next, he turned to Janet: "If you had stayed here, you would have been mine. You still would be if I had not found another. Now that you have chosen him," he looked at Roger with narrow eyes, "you had better get out of the village too!" Roger was by now shaking so hard, the arm that he put around Janet's shoulders to shield her was just as much for his own comfort—he needed something to keep him upright! Lastly, this mighty and intimidating presence turned his eyes on Toby and Roger. "You two are more trouble than you know, and if it had not been for my daughter, you would have been fed to Draugen by now! Yes, you are brave and strong in your way, but to me, you are nothing but a nuisance, and I am weary of dealing with curious and nosy humans, looking for answers. Go away! Leave, and do not come back if you value your short lives! I have spoken!"

The quartet hardly dared to breathe as Axel stared down on the table once more. When animation seeped back into his frame, he looked up, but the smile died on his lips: "What? Why do you stare at me that way?"

"Axel," Toby began, but hearing the shiver in his own voice, he started over again. "Axel, we have listened to a message from someone very old and dangerous, using your body while you were…out? He scared the hell out of us, and that might explain the looks on our faces."

"What?" Axel repeated. Then, looking them in the eyes, he slowly nodded: "It is not the first time something like this has happened to me, I have been used as a medium before, by various spirits, but who was it this time?"

"Njord…" Sandra nearly whispered. "It was Njord. And he was angry. We must leave the area as fast as possible!"

"Njord?" Axel's eyebrows nearly disappeared into his hair, but when he saw their faces, he knew they were being both sincere and truthful.

He sat there without speaking for what seemed like a very long time. Then he looked each of them in the eyes and spoke again: "I am very sorry that you were scared like that. You have had enough scares to last a lifetime for most people, and my intention with coming here, was not just to check on you, but to give you a green light to get out. The police have finished the investigation into Kenneth Barker's death, and we have not got any evidence of foul play. Well, not normal anyway. We have got some problems pinning down the paranormal evidence, although the gadgets and recording devices have scientists from his department in Scotland falling over themselves." He got up and taking his jacket from the back of the chair, thanked Janet for the coffee and bid them all good luck in their future endeavours, wherever they might lead them. Toby, who had been very still these last minutes, now stood up and came over to Axel, giving him a bear hug of his own: "Thank you for coming out this way to see us, we are thankful for both the message and the consideration. You could not know that you were carrying a passenger with a less benevolent message, but no matter what, I am glad to know you!" Axel hugged him back, smiling with suspiciously shiny eyes. Then he bid them all farewell and disappeared out of their lives.

Three days later the texts and phone messages began to taper off. There had been a coup in the Middle East and a school shooting in the USA, so the public interest in the happenings were beginning to taper off. When it was ten days since Mr Peregrine's death, they dared to re-emerge from their hideout, and drive stealthily back to the village. Because they chose a time when very few people were out and about, and also because the weather was appalling at the time, no one noticed their arrival. The next day they were occupied with the packing and cleaning out of their respective houses, and then they were more or less ready to go, they just wanted to speak to Bridget once more, to thank her and to inform her about the conclusion to their adventure.

Chapter 12

Speaking to Bridget proved to be difficult, as she had left the village and had no intention of coming back. That was what the taxi driver told Toby when he was standing in front of the shop, completely lost, as the door was locked, and the windows were dark. The taxi driver, who seemed to be very well informed, said that Bridget had left over a week ago, to stay with a niece in the nearby town, before leaving the village for good. Walking back to Sandra's flat, which was where he was staying now, he had decided to stop by and have a good chat with Bridget, a proper goodbye, so to speak, on his way from Nordheim. He felt a pang of sorrow at the thought of it being for good, but then he remembered the eyes of Njord, and any regrets he had had about leaving swiftly, vanished. Another loose end was Olaf's house, or Toby's, which he was now planning to sell. He had meant to keep it, but with the development that had taken place during his short stay, he would not even want his great-grandchildren to live here. When he thought about it, he would not really have a problem selling it, though. The shortage of housing in the area was acute, and he was confident he was going to get a good price for it. Old houses with what the real estate agents called 'soul' were hot items on the market.

Sandra was also tying off loose ends, as it were. Tidying up her workspace in the library, she spoke for a while with Sissel who had some things to say about the way people were treated in Nordheim. Sissel had always found it a nice place with charming and tolerant people, but now she was forced to reconsider her thinking. The gossip around the village had been humongous, and it was downright nasty what was being said. The gossip mongers had been so busy, she was wondering how they could have time for sleep! And the stories that they told...Sandra agreed to what Sissel said, but she felt detached from it all, like it had happened to someone else. And in a way, it had. She was not the same as she had been, but what she had become would take some time to surface, or at least that was how she felt it, how they all felt it. They had talked this over, all four of them, and they all agreed: they had changed, or been changed, and they hoped it was for the better, but they really could not tell, not yet.

She thought of Janet, who was on sick leave until her resignation had been processed: Boy, she was lucky to have found Roger! He had become a very sturdy and trustworthy man, strong and protective, which was what Janet had always wanted, and now needed, desperately.

Said Roger had perhaps the hardest task of them all. He had to inform his parents about his decisions regarding the farm of which he was the heir, and what he was going to do with his future. First of all, he was going to let his brother, next in line, inherit the farm, thus getting out of a, to him, bleak future. Secondly, he would be leaving town rather immediately, and he saw no chance of himself returning. He had finally decided what he wanted to do with his life, and who he wanted to share it with, so he would be going to another part of the country—probably the east—pursue a training as teacher, and work together with Janet, preferably at the same school. His parents, though saddened by his decision, had respect for it, and they also told Roger in confidence that they were considering selling the farm and moving to the place where his mother came from. Roger was not shocked at the news, he knew what they had been through these last two weeks, and he knew that their trust in their neighbours had been seriously damaged. His brother, they explained, had been losing interest in the wake of the events and how his family had been treated. He had actually been in a couple of fistfights, both on behalf of Roger and on behalf of his parents, so he did not view Nordheim with a favourable eye. There was one thing that made them all happy, though: That Roger and Janet had found each other! That was the best news in a whole year of Mondays, according to his father!

That evening they met up in the pub, all four of them, and found a booth—in the back, as usual—and sat down. There they spent the evening, talking softly about what they were finished with, and if they were ready to leave soon. It did not take them long to find out that they could indeed leave the next day, and as soon as they made the decision, it felt as if a huge weight was lifted off their shoulders. Roger told them about his meeting with his parents and how that had passed, while Janet held his hand and smiled. Toby sat with his arm around Sandra's shoulders, and she was leaning her head on his shoulder, being comforted and comforting him in return.

They spent some time talking about the immediate future, which for Roger and Janet meant relocating to the east and starting a new life there. It was applauded by the other two, after which Janet asked: "What about you? Where will you go and what will you do?" Sandra and Toby looked at each other and then back at Janet and Roger, who both were looking genuinely curious. "We will be going abroad." Sandra said, "Probably to Scotland, perhaps even the Hebrides. We need to try something completely new and start over in a place where nobody knows us and where the media cannot find us. Not without looking very long and hard, anyway!" Roger and Janet were slightly shocked at that, but when they thought about it, they found it to be a very good idea: "And just think of the jolly times we will have, visiting you!" laughed Roger. Now that they had made the decisions that they had been postponing, they felt almost lightheaded, and it was a much livelier group that went home that night. Finally, they would get the peace of mind that had so sorely been eluding them these last two weeks.

On their way out of the pub they met Thor and Ansgar on their way in. After a few seconds of what could be called an uncomfortable silence, Toby broke the ice by exclaiming: "Two of my favourite sunrays! Then I got to wish you farewell after all!" Thor and Ansgar were both dumbstruck at that, but only for a second or two, then they brightened up like the suns Toby had just likened them to, and the farewell the four friends got, was hearty and honestly meant. When they were about to part ways, Ansgar asked Roger in an offhand way if he had seen or spoken with Sofie lately, but Roger answered in the negative. As they stood for a moment out there on the street, ready to go home and finish their packing, he smiled at Toby: "Well, he is still shooting for the moon. Sofie was never interested in him, or anyone else for that matter. Actually, I have never seen a man who claimed her attention for more than a minute or two!" They all laughed at that, and went off to bed, ready for the next day, their last in Nordheim.

In her bed, unable to sleep for the fifth night in a week, Mrs Reignan was fuming. Oh, those insolent, little devils! She had seen them, meeting up outside that awful place, before going in and drowning themselves in alcohol, that devil's water! She was gnashing her teeth, which was not doing them, or her, any good, and pulling at the bedsheet with both hands. So angry was she, that he was in fact pulling it apart. Her whole body was rigid and taut, and her head felt like it was going to explode: She wanted to tell them, she needed to get back at them, she urged for revenge! And then she thought of Mr Peregrine and his hands…how she had longed for those hands to rest on her shoulders, while those remarkable eyes looked into her soul…and now they never would, and it was all the fault of those devil spawned creatures. She hated them, hated their guts!

The next morning, the foursome met up outside Janet's place, loading all their belongings into the back of her van. She had originally bought it to take her students on outings, which made her feel incredibly foresighted now, as it held them all plus their luggage, just barely. On the drive through Nordheim, they all tried to store all the sights in their memories, while at the same time avoiding all the staring, inquisitive, and dark looks they were given on their way. At the ferry quay, Janet parked the car in the marked lane, and stopped it, and they all got out while they waited for the ferry to start loading. Sandra was still, looking into the back of the car, so Toby walked over to her, laid his arms around her, and hugged her from behind: "What is on your mind?" he asked, kissing the top of her head. "I was just thinking about what we bring with us," she answered, "those little things, what we have been packing and repacking, finding space for, somehow. While the biggest thing is in our heads and our memories and might never leave us, unlike that small stuff..." She leaned her head back and looked up into his eyes: "Am I making sense to you, or did that sound as confused as I feel?"

"It did make sense, and I suppose it will make even more sense to us when we get some distance between this and us," he answered, then hugged her again. The ferry came to life now, the engine starting up and the crew aboard coming up to start the loading process. Janet got in the car, while the other three stood there, ready to start walking on board.

A crowd of people suddenly appeared between the cars, marching toward them, looking rather aggressive in their body language and quite clearly meaning business. Roger and Sandra looked at each other, then at Toby, with facial expressions that spoke their minds clearly: "Oh, no! Not again...This is not what we need!" Sandra had tears in her eyes. Toby was looking at the coming 'parade of upstanding citizens' as she could have sworn, she heard him mutter under his breath. Then he gave her a real bear hug, nodded to Roger, and told them to get on the ferry and wait for him. "It will not take me long to say 'Goodbye' to these sweet and charitable people, who have come to see us safely on our way!" This last was said in a rather loud tone, so that everyone present, including the said people, heard it clearly. Some of the good church club members even blushed a little. But not Mrs Reignan. She was walking in front of the club, marching with determined and measured steps, with a fire in her eyes, and heart, Toby guessed. Stopping in front of him, with the precision of a military cohort, she looked at him with a face that needed no words: she detested him, loathed him, and if she could have traded John Peregrine out of hell by selling Toby's soul, she would have done just that.

Fixing him in her icy stare, as she was used to, she began delivering her farewell speech: "Leave, and if you are thinking of coming back, stay away! You are not welcome! You never have been. You are responsible for everything bad and evil that has happened in this peaceful place, and the faster you disappear, the faster things will go back to normal, and we may resume our lives and mourn the one we have lost with dignity! Despicable demon spawn, go back to wherever you crawled out from, I curse the day you arrived here!" Stopping to catch her breath, she was surprised and shocked when Toby, his face now completely still, but with anger written all over it, stepped forward toward her. Mrs Reignan backed away and almost stumbled, suddenly terrified for herself, thinking: "My Lord, he is going to hit me!" But Toby was not the man to hit even a rabid dog like Mrs Reignan. Instead, he spoke up, so loudly that everyone, not just the people standing closest, could hear him. "Do not worry, I am not going to hit you. I would not sully myself that way. I just wanted a good, hard look at what intolerable self-righteousness looks like. So that, in case I am unfortunate enough to meet it in another place, I will know how it looks, and take a detour! You made my grandfather's life miserable, or at least you tried to. Know that he was laughing at your attempts, in fact: he still is laughing, both hard and long. For that alone you had deserved to be put in the pillory, but you have added to your crimes since then. Or what?" Mrs Reignan was in a state of shock, and therefore unable to answer him, and as for the rest? Well, they were either flabbergasted that someone would dare tell her off like this, or secretly agreeing with Toby, and therefore not saying anything. Toby's final farewell, as he turned to go on board, left them dumfounded while Mrs Reignan hyperventilated and collapsed: "I will not worry about meeting you again, no fate could be that cruel. No matter what religion you adhere to, they all have a special place prepared for people like you, and it is not the one with the harps in it!" He then went aboard the ferry, with a spring in his step that had not been there since he came to Nordheim, perhaps never, if truth be told.

Sandra welcomed him with open arms and a laughing smile: "You were simply wonderful!" Together the four friends stood there on deck and watched as Nordheim slipped away from them, the glacier shining like a diamond, and all the colours sparkling and mirroring themselves in the fjord.

The last image he ever got of that pearl of the fjords, was the glacier, mountains, rivers, and forests lying there as peaceful as ever, while a dark, threatening mass of clouds rose dramatically over the mountains and glacier in the north.

Sofie had been at the quay and witnessed Toby's final farewell to Mrs Reignan and her cronies, and like many others, she was secretly laughing and cheering him on. On her way home, she tried to stop at the store, only to realise that it was still closed, although there were rumours that it had been sold. When she walked into her house, it was with a decisive spring in her steps. She walked up the stairs and into her bedroom where she undressed and then put on a pretty, white dress and sandals.

Coming back downstairs, she paused and looked in the mirror in the hall, checking her hair and putting on some discrete make-up: just mascara and a little lip gloss, that was all she needed, really. Walking out the door and closing it behind her, she had the appearance of a young woman on her first date, happily anticipating an evening of total bliss. Anyone who saw her, would see it immediately: this was a woman in love! She slipped onto a lane, going up towards the mountain side, in the direction of the cliff that had been so much in the public eye for the last weeks.

Walking lazily along the lane, she was smiling secretly and singing softly to herself. The lane soon turned into a path, climbing steeply up until she reached her goal, high up there. She turned to take in the view like so many tourists had done before, and in that moment, if you had looked her in the eyes, you would not have recognised her.

Then she turned her back on the village and was never seen nor heard from again.

Travelling first to the town where Toby signed the last papers with the real-estate agency and made arrangements for how the resulting sum from the sale should be handled, they next went in search of Bridget's niece. They did find her in the end, but they were too late to meet up with Bridget, as she had travelled on the day before. When the niece, a very kind and smiling young lady, saw how disappointed they became, she first invited them to sit down and have a cup of coffee with her. Then she went into the house, and when she came back, she was carrying gifts in her arms, which she divided out among them. For Roger, there were several books, all about teaching, Zen, and fly-fishing! Roger just sat there and looked at them, half smiling, half blushing. For Janet, there was a basket filled with all kinds of herbs and spices, which she could put to good use. Janet shone like the evening sun when she received it. For Toby, there was only one book, but it was big, both in size and in content. It was Olaf's work, made from the years of research, with countless tales, observations, and theories in it. It was a wonder of a book, and it left Toby leaking from the eyes, unable to say a single word. Lastly, she turned to Sandra. Holding a heavy bundle, she read out from a card that was attached to it: "For you I have something special, a gift that can only be given once in your life, and only to your true heir. Use it well and with care, and may it bring you blessings as it has me. Love, Bridget." Then she handed the bundle to Sandra, who opened it carefully, went pale and wide eyed in shock, and quickly closed the bundle to protect it from prying eyes. When the others looked questioningly at her, she told them, with a little quiver in her voice: "It is her book, The Book of Shadows, the big book we saw her fetch when she taught us how to escape Njord."

"Oh…" came the reply from three stunned friends around the table.

Before leaving her, they thanked the niece, who was also named Bridget, for the gifts and the help she had given them. They had been given the address to where Bridget would be staying for a while, down in Bergen, and they were going there to talk with her before they went their separate ways. Now, only one thing remained to do, before they could leave the area for good: they had to say goodbye to Axel Hoegh. But they found that even more difficult than finding Bridget. The receptionist at the police station, just sat there looking nonplussed when they asked for him. Then he called for another, more senior officer, but he also looked completely blank. Roger was beginning to wonder what on earth was going on, when the police chief entered the room. He was a good-natured, smiling man, and so he deeply regretted having to tell them that Axel Hoegh passed away a couple of years earlier, disappearing in the mountains of Nordheim, and never having been found. The only thing they ever discovered of his possessions, were some fishing tackles and his boots, lying by the mountain lake where he had been fishing. Toby wanted to scream, and he could tell that the others were close to freaking out as well, but somehow, he managed to keep his face and voice steady when he told the officer how sorry he was. They then all took their leave, and fighting furiously to keep their cool, left as quick as they could, without raising suspicion.

Back in the car, they gave in to hysteria, and for some minutes everything was complete chaos. When they managed to calm down, Roger was the first to speak, and what he said, made the rest of them nod in agreement. "Norway is not safe for us. Scandinavia is not safe for us. In fact, Europe might not be safe, but we will have to go somewhere, so I think we will be joining you in Scotland."

"Yes," echoed Janet, "if you will take us with you?"

"Why do you ask, it is a no-brainer!" replied Toby and Sandra in tandem. Settling in their seats, they started the trip into the unknown, as far as they were concerned.

Two days later, they were sitting round the coffee table in Bridget's small flat in Bergen, smiling and talking, while consuming beer, whisky, and pizza, in that order. Bridget seemed the same as always, friendly, smiling, good-humoured, with a heart-warming laughter at the ready. Yet, something was off, both Toby and Sandra sensed it: Something was wrong and was bothering her, but what? Finally, they had to ask her, and it was Sandra who voiced their concern: "Bridget, what is the matter? You seem yourself, but we can see that something is weighing on your mind!" The answer was shocking in its intensity, although they did not understand it at the time: "Have you had contact with your family lately, Roger?"

"Yes," he affirmed, "and they bid me say hello to you when we saw you."

"That is awfully nice of them, you must thank them when you talk to them again," she said, but then she continued: "I am worried for them. Do they intend to stay on in that poisoned environment?" Roger looked around at the other three. He had told them what his parents intended to do, but he had not told them what his father had said when they talked on the phone the night before.

Now, however, he did: "No, they do not. They have finally sold the farm to one of our neighbours, and are moving to my mother's hometown, the moving van will be there tomorrow. My brother is leaving with them, he has had enough of Nordheim to last him a lifetime!" If they had expected Bridget to be upset with the news, they were wrong. She smiled, a real, genuine smile this time, and visibly relaxed. Roger was just sitting there, now that he had let the cat out of the bag, so to speak, but he was clearly troubled about something else as well. "Come on, young man, no need to let your head hang down!" Bridget was looking at him with a smile in her eyes. "It is my cousin," Roger told them, "Sofie Oldnes. We have never been very close, hanging with different crowds and having nothing to do with each other, really. But now she has gone missing, vanished, and there is absolutely no clue to where she could be!" Bridget, now looking serious, sighed: "Could it be that Sofie has had enough of the goings-on in Nordheim and has decided to skip town for good?" she said. Roger furrowed his brow, then nodded slowly: "It would not be entirely out of character, she has always been wilful." Toby's eyes hazed over: he remembered something the entity that was Njord had said to them, something about Janet…he could not remember, at least not at present. Then he looked up and met Bridget's eyes, serious and sad. She shook her head almost imperceptibly, and indicated that he should hold his tongue, which he did: there was no sense in stirring up more emotions when there was nothing any living person could do about it.

Roger still looked uneasy, though, and after some prompting by Bridget, he sighed. Lifting his eyes up and meeting hers, Roger then voiced what they all secretly feared: "Was it our fault? Everything that happened, the death of Kenneth, of Mr Peregrine, the division that surfaced in the village, was that our doing?" Bridget looked around at all of them, seeing the same question in four pairs of eyes, noticing the desperation in their faces, and then she sighed: "No! It is not, nor was it ever, your fault. You all followed what you had been taught, your own good sense, and your sense of what was right, and you did it all in honesty and earnestness. Which is why Froya helped you: she appreciates honesty and love, and she is always opposed to lies and falsehoods. The presence of Njord himself in human form was and is scary, but it also shows that he has a healthy respect for you, do not forget that! The people who have something to fear, the people who stirred his anger, are the ones that will have to bear the brunt of it when he takes out his revenge. Fortunately, you have all left, and will not be hit by it." She held each one of them in her gaze for some seconds, then she relaxed with a sigh, and sat back in her chair: "So when are you leaving?" Toby told her of their plans, which had solidified since their departure from Nordheim: "We are first going to Edinburgh, where we will meet up with a representative from an agency that supplies teachers to schools in the Outer Hebrides. He was overjoyed at getting four able teachers in the same group and was ready to put us on a boat before we got there, almost! He was talking of two different locations where they were in desperate need of someone to come in take over the school, but I think he landed on North Uist. Which means we will be learning Scottish Gaelic, by the way!"

"Oh, dear me, that will be a mouthful!" laughed Bridget.

They sat there, revelling in the company of friends and hesitant to say "Goodbye," but all good things come to an end, and at last they had to go. The boat that would take them to Scotland, left at eight o'clock the following morning, and had boarding hours at 0700, so they needed to go to bed relatively early. Standing there outside, they suddenly found it difficult to speak, but then Bridget broke the tension: "Oh, come on, what is this, a funeral?!? We will meet again, when you least expect it, but now the time for parting has come. You must go on to your new adventure, and I must take some much-needed rest after our last. But, believe me, you have not seen the last of me!" That was the signal for a lot of hugging, after which they began their walk back to the hotel. The next morning, they went to the departure dock, and boarded the boat that would take them, in Bridget's words, on to a new adventure. Standing there on deck, feeling the ship's motors starting to propel them away, they felt a pang of sorrow for what they could have had, but then it passed. Slowly, they turned their backs to the shore, and went inside.

When they arrived in Scotland, they felt a little bit as if they had landed in a roller-coaster ride: The agent, Angus

Brenna, whom Toby had spoken with, was as good as his word. He had them settled with contracts, work permits, and was ready to help them apply for citizenship, before they were finished with the initial "Hello, how are you?" The next day, after shopping all the essentials, and more of the things they did not need, but found that they wanted, anyway, they were on a plane, headed for North Uist, or Uibhist a Tuath in Scottish Gaelic, where the school year would start in three weeks' time. "Plenty of time to learn a new, old language!" Roger groaned.

Fortunately, the houses that had been found for them, were adjacent to one another, and although old, they were well insulated and incredibly cosy and snug. They settled into their new situation surprisingly fast, and they were warmly welcomed by the islanders.

Some days later, while sitting in the tiny lounge at their new workplace: a small school in the town of Lochmaddy on the east coast of North Uist, Roger suddenly exclaimed: "NO!" making the other three almost jump out of their chairs. "What?!" said Sandra and Janet together, while Toby just stared at Roger, noticing how all colour slowly drained from his face, and getting a sinking feeling in his stomach. "This…" whispered Roger and turned his tablet for all of them to read, while their faces began to resemble his.

"NTB: Nordheim, one of our biggest tourist destinations, was literally obliterated today in a surprise mountain slide that caused a tsunami almost 30 metres high and wiped out the community in its entirety. It is a devastating shock for everyone who has heard of or ever been to this incredibly beautiful pearl of the western fjords. The tsunami then travelled out the fjord and has also caused substantial damage along the main fjord, with many villages and tourist destinations left devastated. How many who have lost their lives, is yet to be ascertained, but it is feared that the number is high. The whole nation is in shock and deep sorrow."

The Thundering Silence

Location: Nordheim, village/town by a side arm of the Sognefjord under the glacier.

Population: Around 300 citizens, two hotels, a pub, a post office, a doctor's office, a village school (1st through 10th grade), lots of tourism, one grocery (all-things) store, many large (and small) book shops, a library, a community house, an indoor shooting range, as well as an outdoor one, and a winter sports arena.

Characters in the book:

- Olaf Larsen—recently deceased, in his eighties, retired farmer and fisherman, and an authority in the field of old superstitions, ancient gods, and paranormal beings and occurrences. He had—in the minds of the other villagers—some wild ideas about this issue, and these grew more and more outrageous as the years went by.
- Toby Larsen—late twenties, descendant of (grandson) and heir to Olaf, the local 'personality' (weirdo).

- Roger Brigstad—late twenties, relative of Toby, great-grandson of Thormod, Olaf's cousin.
- Sandra Billings—late twenties, friend of Olaf, sharing the same or similar ideas, an accomplished witch.
- Kenneth Barker—ghost hunter and paranormal researcher.
- Janet Johnston—in her early thirties, teacher.
- Bridget Waters—mid seventies, store owner.
- Sofie Oldnes—local farmer, in her late twenties, distant cousin of Roger's.
- Sissel Davik—librarian in her 40s, friend of Sandra.
- Thor Dalen—friend of Roger, regular at the pub.
- Ansgar Vik—friend of Roger, regular at the pub.
- Axel Hoegh—police officer (very tall and broad: 6 ft 8).
- John Peregrine—early sixties, village priest (busybody and know-it-all).
- Mrs (Charlotte) Reignan—widow, in her early sixties, sharp faced and with an acid tongue, avid supporter of Mr Peregrine, member of the church club.
- Mrs Eleanora Kingsman—mid fifties, proprietor of the Hotel Daleswood, member of the church club.
- Mr Jeremy Rowan—late forties, proprietor of the Fjordsuite Hotel, member of the church club.
- Mr Jonathan Starby—in his late fifties, wealthy farmer, member of the church club.
- Mrs Amelia Thornson—member of the church club.
- Mrs Ruth Thorsten—member of the church club.

Ingram Content Group UK Ltd.
Milton Keynes UK
UKHW021545070623
423041UK00012B/619